Bourbon Street Blues
and
The Green Wave

Bourbon Street Blues and The Green Wave

A Novel

William A. Miller

ZONE PRESS
Denton, Texas

Bourbon Street Blues and The Green Wave
By William A. Miller

No part of this book may be reproduced or transmitted in any form or by any means, graphic, electronic, or mechanical, including photocopying, recording, taping, or by any information storage retrieval system, without the permission in writing from the publisher.

All Rights Reserved © 2004 by William A. Miller

Zone Press
an imprint of Rogers Publishing and Consulting, Inc.
109 East Oak – Suite 300
Denton, Texas 76201
info@zonepress.com

Jim O. Rogers - Editor
Charlotte Beckham - Copy Edit
Lori Walker - Production and Design
Jim O. Rogers - Cover Design

Any resemblance to actual people and events is purely coincidental. This is a work of fiction.

Printed in the United States of America
ISBN:0-9761706-3-9

Dedication
▼ ▼ ▼

This book is dedicated to Ellie Peterson Miller, my loving wife who shared the writing experience with me.

CREDITS
▼▼▼

Writings in Michael Ondaatje's book, *Coming Through Slaughter,* Random House, N.Y., gave assurance of authenticity of early New Orleans Jazz musicians, especially Buddy Bolden.

Prologue
▼▼▼

Kate peeked from behind the maroon satin curtain. A leg teased forward. The rattle of a cowbell sounded from the band. She strode out from behind the curtain as Buddy's band swung into full gear. She undulated around the stage, a rhythmic, pulsating, cakewalkin' Creole baby. Her svelte full thighs rotated in time to the music above tapered knees, slim calves and ankles. Her flowing black hair partially covered sultry brown eyes and pouty lips. Sweat stained a barely distinguishable G-string on this struttin' gal at Lulu White's Mahogany Hall on Basin Street in New Orleans. Kate was her name, and dancin' was her game.

The smell of stale beer enveloped a steamy smoke-filled Mahogany Hall where eager yet subdued patrons gathered at stageside enjoying the show, already anticipating Kate's next dance.

"I Wish I Could Shimmy Like My Sister Kate," provided the background for the performance. Buddy Bolden's cornet bit the air shrilly enough that the night watchman could hear the wail 10 miles away at Lake Ponchatrain.

She glided to the right side of the stage in a slow cakewalk that caused her delicious body to shake. She paused at the corner of the stage slightly before quickening the pace and striding to the other side.

Finally, she positioned herself in the middle of the stage with her back to the still-gathering crowd. Deftly, she discarded a tasseled top. In perfect unison with the band's beat, she slowly turned with demure arms covering her ample bosom. Should she—or should she not? The cowbell rang. In a flash, she did. The audience gasped.

She came front and center and teased a mock removal of the G-string. The crowd cheered enthusiastically as Kate shimmied and shook toward the curtain to a closing gutbucket rendition of "Sister Kate". With a backward wink, she exited, and Buddy moved on to his next number, "Tin Roof Blues."

Buddy (Kid) Bolden, wearing black pants, red shirt and white suspenders punched and drove his cornet. Willie Cornish trailed and wailed the valve trombone, echoing Buddy's every move. Frank Lewis floated above them all in a clarinet rhapsody. Brock Mumford's guitar strung out a slow drag. Cornelius Tilman rattled the drums in slow march cadence. Jimmy Johnson kept it all together with the thump, thump of his bass, and Alcide Frank played a lyricial counterpoint on his violin.

Buddy had invited Bunk Johnson, a young cornet virtuoso, to join in the fun on this particular night; and Bunk found his way as second cornet.

Tom Anderson patronized Buddy Bolden with money and booze. Buddy cut hair during the day at N. Joseph's Shaving Parlor and played his blazing cornet at night. Buddy talked big during the day as he administered a shave and a haircut for six bits. Brothel wallpaper, fit only to cover the walls of Lulu White's Mahogany Hall, adorned the shaving parlor walls. Shaves were best gotten before noon as Buddy grew increasingly loose and tipsy as the day wore on.

A writer had it that Buddy Bolden was the best, loudest and most loved Jazzman of his time, but never professional in the brain. Unconcerned with the crack of the lip, he threw out and held immense notes, and could reach a first note in seconds that violently assaulted the ear. The side of his mouth dragged a net of air into his lungs, dressed it up in notes and poured it out again in the night air. He made the notes last and last as if he yearned to leave them hanging up there in the sky like air transformed into clouds…

Bunk Johnson had gone to Lincoln Park that hot Louisiana night to hear Buddy Bolden, whose band had the whole of New Orleans crazy, running wild behind it. Bolden looked down at the youngster as he stood there, with his cornet in a green cloth cover under his arm, and said, "What you got there, Boy?"

Bunk said, "A cornet."

Bolden asked, "Can you play it?"

"I can play it." Bunk nodded, confident.

"Can you play the Blues, Boy?" Bolden drew on a near-burned out cigarette.

"I can play the Blues," said Bunk, jutting out his chin.

"What key you play the Blues in?" Bolden persisted.

"Any key you've got," Bunk answered. And he did. And that's how he got to play second cornet with King Bolden's Band.

Such was life in Storyville during the early 20th Century.

Sports and ladies of the evening met and blended in a delicious, sensual dance on Bourbon Street, down New Orleans way.

On the front door of Madam Tonia's, a mansion operated by Antonia Gonzalez, read an inscription entitled "Gonzalez Female Cornet Player."

Mayor Tom Anderson kept a record of dancers and ladies in the district's city hall. Ragtime piano professors, string trios, and small jazz or spasm bands pounded out the music. Tony Jackson played a wide range of songs from the Blues to operatic arias; however, the Blues naked dances were his most famous work.

Famous names like Buddy Bolden, Joe Oliver, Freddie Keppard, Louis Armstrong, pioneer tailgating trombonist Ed (Kid) Ory and the jazz composer, pianist Ferdinand Joseph (Jelly Roll) Morton performed in sporting houses and Honky Tonks along the waterfront. The ragtime piano and New Orleans brass bands developed simultaneously out of the bubbling caldron of humanity. Here comes The Old Excelsior Brass Band struttin' down Rampart Street to "Take Your Big Leg Off of Me."

The word "Dixie" comes from New Orleans. New Orleans was commercial center of the South before the Louisiana Purchase. Legal tender was issued in French/English. Most prominent was the ten dollar issue. Ten in French is dix which was printed in large letters on back of the bill. The New Orleans region became known as the land of "dixies" or "Dixieland." Buddy Bolden was the earliest lead cornetist playing Dixie rags, blues, stomps, hymns, marches, waltzes, quadrilles and chants. All of this merged with the confluence of cultures (French, Spanish, African, English and Caribbean) into what is today known as Dixieland Jazz.

CHAPTER 1
▼▼▼

Dixieland Jazz etched an indelible impression on Zach LaSalle's brain at the tender age of nine. It was 1937. Zach's parents had taken him to watch a basketball game at Texas Wesleyan College in Fort Worth. He never forgot it. Sandy Sandifur wailed "Sugar Blues" and "Tiger Rag" until it brought tears to Zach's eyes. Basketball and jazz pep bands blended together like they were made for each other, thought Zach. A marvelously artistic and aesthetically pleasing connection was seared into Zach's heart. He was never quite the same afterward.

Zach wanted to play a trumpet like Sandy Sandifur, and play basketball like Easy Parham. His parents purchased a silver Conn trumpet for him on his 10th birthday. The first tune he learned was "Mary Had a Little Lamb." Zach's parents soon grew tired of the tune. No doubt, they regretted their purchase at times. Mostly hot air and not much music came out of his horn, early on.

In 1940 at age 12, Zach played second trumpet in the Fort

Worth Junior Symphony Orchestra. He never achieved first chair because of a fellow named Gordon Moore.

"Let us try this passage over," said the youth orchestra conductor. "And Mr. LaSalle, please play on key."

Gordon Moore was so good he could play 'off key' on purpose. The conductor thought it was Zach and that he didn't know any better. In Fort Worth, Zach learned about jazz and classical music.

In 1943, Zach moved to Dallas and started acquiring jazz records from record stores, religiously. Collections by early New Orleans musicians included Bunk Johnson, Kid Ory, and George Lewis. Zach also had collections by Muggsy Spanier's Ragtime Band, Pete Daily's Dixieland Band, and Lu Watter's Yerba Buena Jazz Band from out San Francisco way. He could never play a trumpet like Sandy Sandifur, or basketball like Easy Parham, but he never stopped trying.

Chapter 2
▼▼▼

The big war had ended the previous year, and in December of 1946 Zach LaSalle settled into his seat on the Burlington Zephyr in Dallas and headed for New Orleans, Louisiana. At age 19, he played basketball on a scholarship for Tulane University.

Two hundred and sixty-three years earlier his namesake Robert Cavalier de LaSalle led an expedition of 56 persons down the Mississippi River to the Gulf of Mexico. He disembarked, built a monument and inscribed on it the Coat of Arms of King Louis XIV of France. He named the region Louisiana.

The Burlington Zephyr passed over the Sabine River and rocked and rolled its way toward New Orleans. Soldiers and sailors crowded the lurching train. The air smelled stale with cigarette smoke and sweaty poker players swilling gin. Zach had missed serving in the war by six months. He felt a little bit out of place with all the young men in uniform. Most of the soldiers peered quietly out the windows, deep in thought.

Zach turned to his seatmate. "Are you headed for New

Orleans?" he inquired.

"Name's Sergeant Polk, and I'm headed for Biloxi. What's your name?"

"LaSalle, Zach LaSalle. Came up to visit my parents, and now I'm going back."

Polk queried, "You going down to have some fun in the Big Easy? No telling what you'll run into. All those queens with flashing eyes might be a bit too tough for you." Sergeant Polk lifted a package of Camels from his starched khaki shirt, knocked one loose, and bounced it vigorously off his watch.

Zach had acquired a taste for cigars and recently had purchased his first cigar lighter. Wanting to appear suave, he fired up his lighter and reached over to oblige the Sergeant with a light.

Polk nodded, "Thanks," then took a deep drag and waited for the hair in his singed nostrils to quit burning. "That's a hell of a flame thrower you got there. We could have torched half of the German army with that thing."

Embarrassment crept up Zach's neck. He had wanted to be one of the boys, which he obviously wasn't.

"Sandwiches, chips, milk, candy. Wha da ya want?" shrilled the male vendor coming down the aisle. He was doing a brisk business.

Zach reached into the pocket of his Levis and pulled out a dollar bill that would nicely purchase his evening meal.

The sun made its low arc, shining through the train windows on the hazy winter day. It would soon pass completely below the horizon.

When dusk fell, Zach made his way to the trailing lounge car and ran into Sergeant Polk once more.

"How about a beer, young man? You like Jax or Schlitz?"

"Thanks, I'll take a Schlitz." Zach liked the brown label on the bottle.

A porter in starched white linen handed Zach a cold bottle. Sergeant Polk had already plunked down a fifty-cent piece. With obliging nods, they took swigs and licked their lips. Zach felt a guilty pain hit him. It was, after all, the middle of the basketball season.

A radio was playing Glenn Miller's "String of Pearls" in the background. Zach noticed a box of Roi Tans neatly perched on the makeshift bar. He sprang for two, which put a twenty-cent hole in his pocket.

"Here, Sarge, have one on me," Zach announced with naïve *savoir faire*. He and the Sarge lit up together with the Sarge feigning mock alarm when Zach struck flint to his lethal weapon.

Sarge took another swig and puffed on his stogy. "My feet hurt. Nearly froze them off in the Bulge. You didn't miss anything, young buddy. I'm just glad it's over; and as soon as I get to Biloxi, I'll be mustered out, and go on home to Pensacola."

Over the next few minutes, Zach struck up a friendship with the returning war veteran – one of many who had fought so valiantly. They talked for a while.

"Take care pal, and stay out of trouble down New Orleans way." With a parting nod to Zach, Sergeant Polk opened the compartment door to return to his coach seat. The roar of the tracks and a faint odor of acrid train smoke entered the lounge car. Then the door shut. The lounge car began to empty out except for a young lady who gazed demurely out the lounge car window. Occasionally she cast furtive glances in Zach's direction. She wore an apricot organza dress that revealed a shapely but delicate figure. Zach sat mesmerized by the honey brown tone of her skin. As if in private agreement, they departed the lounge car together.

"Hi," said Zach.

"*Bonjour,*" came the reply.

Their bodies brushed as they eased out onto the platform. The night air bit momentarily; but it passed quickly as they entered the coach car, which swayed back and forth gently. She sat down across from Zach. It was late and a couple of beers had passed Zach's lips, leaving him in a relaxed mood. A porter passed out pillows for the long night ahead. Zach took one and attempted to adjust his head against the zigzagging window ledge. Too rough. He positioned it against the back of the seat and cradled his head in it. A glance told him that the young mystery lady was having trouble negotiating her pillow. "Here, let me help you," he eagerly intoned while catching his breath from the faint hint of her fragrant perfume.

"Thank you, and who are you?" She extended a graceful hand.

"Zach LaSalle, from Dallas," he announced, proudly.

She glanced down and surveyed his shiny, lizard-skin western boots peeking out from under starched Levis. Zach was no cowboy, but he was a good football and basketball player. He wasn't a bad musician either; at the tender age of 16 he had fronted a Dixieland jazz band in Deep Ellum in Dallas. They were called the Razzmatazz Boys. Tom Knighton was the drummer; Charlie McDaniel, trombone; and Charlie Bell was the clarinetist.

"And what is your name?"

"Marie Tranchepaine, of New Orleans. I am returning to New Orleans from a visit with friends in Dallas."

"I'm on my way back to New Orleans. Been home for a couple of Christmas days. Gotta get back to basketball practice tomorrow. Cuttin' it pretty close."

"Basketball practice?" asked Marie.

"Yeah, I play for Tulane. You ever watch college basketball?"

"Not very much. I go to school at Loyola. We are neighbors."

"I have never been on that campus, and it's just up the street from Tulane."

"I have a Pullman sleeper, but I'm so tired, I think I will just stay here tonight. It's a long walk to the sleeper," said Marie, sitting up with her head encased in the pillow that Zach had arranged. She closed her eyes.

Zach studied Marie for a few minutes. He liked the way her hair curled against her cheek. Soon sleep overtook him.

Chapter 3
▼▼▼

Zach awakened when the train came to a grinding stop. It was pitch dark outside. Zach looked at the florescent hands on his watch. 4 a.m. He could hear the distant clanging of cars being unhitched and hitched. The noise grew closer; then his car bumped harshly, tossing Zach into Marie who was now awake, too.

"What in the world is happening?" intoned a sleepy, stretching Marie.

Zach peered out the window. He could see lanterns swinging to and fro. "I don't have a clue."

Bang-bang, and soon they were drifting forward again. Their car was being ferried across the Mississippi River.

"We're on a barge or something," Zach said, uneasily. The drifting soon came to a stop. Clang-clang, steel on steel. A lantern swung high, and they moved ever so slowly, finally beginning to pick up speed. Clickety-clack, clickety-clack. Once they were underway again, Zach and Marie settled into an uncomfortable fitful sleep. Zach awoke to a crimson gray horizon. The sun was on its way up, and so was Zach.

"Marie, would you like to go get some breakfast?"

She shook her head no, shut her eyes and went back to sleep.

Zach entered the all-purpose car with his shaving gear and toothbrush. Sergeant Polk was halfway through shaving, and Zach sidled up alongside him and ran some water in the tiny metal sink. Zach's beard wasn't all that dense, but he liked the smell of rich sudsy lather. He opened his razor and inserted a new Gillette double-edge blade.

He finished about the same time the Sarge did. They rinsed their faces and dried off with small Burlington towels. A splash of Old Spice after-shave did the trick.

He left the car in which shaving and other necessities took place and walked toward the diner. A long line awaited him. The air filled with burning tobacco smoke. Sailors and soldiers waited side-by-side for their chance at breakfast. Standing between cars, Zach became entranced with the rocking and sliding motion of the metal platform on which he stood. He pulled his letter jacket up around his neck. It was cold outside.

Finally, the line moved forward, and he was again inside. He ordered a small orange juice along with ham and eggs. He seated himself alongside a sailor and across from a marine, both headed for Pensacola. Zach had no way of participating in the small talk. He ate his breakfast and returned to his coach to find Marie fresh and primped, and more alluringly beautiful than ever.

"Thirty minutes estimate arrival time to New Orleans," announced the conductor, making a final check of tickets and passengers.

"May I ask what you are reading?" inquired Zach of Marie.

Marie pushed her reading glasses up off her nose. "Victor Hugo's *Les Miserables*. It's part of my reading assignment for French lit class."

Zach raised his eyebrows. "French lit, huh."

"Yes, I am majoring in English literature, and minoring in French literature. And what are you studying at Tulane?"

Zach hadn't thought he was 'studying' anything in particular, but he did have a leaning toward literature. He liked to read. "I'm taking 15 hours this semester. Algebra, English lit, speech, sociology, and a P.E. course. My most immediate concern is to pass the Algebra class. I might major in English lit. Don't know yet."

Marie matter of factly volunteered, "I am enrolled in the College of Liberal Arts at Loyola."

"Back home liberal is a bad word," said Zach.

Marie attempted to help out. "A liberal education should help free you from ignorance. It is about freedom of thought and expression; acquiring the ability to see many sides to issues and work toward mutually acceptable resolution of differences. Thomas Paine's *Essays on Freedom* is a good starting point. Liberal education is about understanding humanity and progress that should take place regarding humanity. At Loyola, we study certain subjects that will help in this liberation. So there, Mr. Zach, you have it in a nutshell."

Zach thought – nice combination, smart and beautiful. "My favorite subjects are basketball and jazz. What do you think of that?"

"You don't look athletic."

"What are athletes supposed to look like?"

No answer from Marie.

The train had slowed to a crawl and, with creaking brakes and a shudder, stopped. They were in New Orleans Union Station. Zach reached up and pulled his small duffle bag down and helped Marie with her suitcase. They moved toward the rear of the car to make their exit.

"Watch your step," a porter cautioned and held out his hand for Marie.

Zach followed, unassisted.

"It has been a pleasure meeting you." Marie extended her hand.

Zach took Marie's hand, which was soft and smooth to the touch. "The pleasure has been all mine. Can I get you a cab or something?"

Marie responded, "No, but I'll give you a ride out to Tulane if you like."

A long black limousine awaited Marie, and Zach took her up on her offer. Besides, it was a long walk up St. Charles Avenue.

"Martin Maelson, this is Zach LaSalle, a friend of mine, and I would like to give him a ride out to Tulane."

"Whatever you wish, Miss Marie," said Martin, a man of colour, in a pressed black suit and chauffeur's cap.

Zach crawled in after Marie. There was enough room in there to shoot baskets. They moved up Canal Street and over to St. Charles. Ancient moss-covered oaks and lagoons lined the way. Zach sat back, stretched his long legs, and crossed his booted feet.

"You have a horse?" questioned Marie.

"Not with me."

Zach was an L & L man. Lips and legs. Marie was extraordinary in both categories.

As they neared the Tulane campus, Zach said, "We have a basketball game with LSU next week. Would you like to come?"

Marie took a small pad from her purse, and hurriedly wrote Marie de le Tranchepaine, Elegante de Arms, 1938 St. Charles Avenue. Magnolia 444-1. "Call me."

Zach exited the limo, and took her hand. "Thanks for the ride. I'll be seeing you."

Marie watched this lanky Texan throw his duffle bag over his broad shoulder. He turned and hesitated, then smiled, and with a winsome upturned brow gave a little bow and started his walk across the Tulane campus. The tight Levis encased a revealing derriere and slightly bowed legs. He was 6'2" maybe 3", she guessed. He strode along loose and confident.

Chapter 4
▼▼▼

"Martin, would you please drop me by the "Quarter" on the way home?" asked Marie. "I want to pick up an item or two at Madame Pontalbam's Perfume Parlor."

"Yes," replied Martin with courteous affection. "It is on Royale Street, is it not?"

"About the middle of the block."

They passed old Greek revival buildings along Carondelet, and the black limo pulled sharply onto Royale. Marie entered the courtyard, which was completely walled in. A great iron gate closed off the *porte cochere* that led from the street. Flowering vines covered the old brick walls. Pastel blossoms, fern hanging baskets, and camellia bushes accented the *porte*. Marie's slightly raised high heels pattered the uneven bricks. Ah, Marie smiled, pleased. Madam Pontalbam was open for business. Marie smelled the sweet aroma of perfumes that could lead to forbidden pleasures. She rapped gently on the massive door before she proceeded into the inner sanctum. The fragrance of *vetiver* adorned the air; also woodsy and green eucalyptus. There was also a hint of lavender.

"*Ma chère âmie,* do come in. You look lovely as usual. Please have a seat," asserted Madam Pontalbam with expensive hand gestures and raised eyebrows heavily coated with pencil.

"*Bon jour, ma chatte.* Thank you." Marie seated herself demurely on a peach velvet sofa. "Do you have my favorite *Le Jardin de cour parfum?*"

"It is very difficult to get these days, but for you, yes I have the perfect bottle," exclaimed Madam Pontalbam with a hint of smugness. "You are aware, Marie, that Cleopatra snared Mark Antony with this very fragrance. Do you perhaps have a Mark Antony in mind?"

Marie smiled, "Well maybe not quite Mark Antony."

"Oh, someone so special to be treated to *Le Jardin.* My, my."

"Charge it to the Baron, please." Moments later, Marie stepped back into the courtyard, to join a waiting Martin.

She settled into the back seat, kicked off her shoes and laid her head back. The long train ride had tired her, but she felt strangely invigorated by the thought of Zach. What was his last name? LaSalle, if her memory served her correctly. Yes, she definitely wanted him to call.

We are all born for love.
It is the principle of existence
And its only end.
--Disraeli—Sybil. Bk. 5 Ch. 4.

CHAPTER 5
▼▼▼

Zach settled back into the athletic dorm. His best friend, a fellow forward on the basketball team, Neil Jackson, waited there for him. The redhead was a descendant of the Irish who settled in New Orleans the middle of the 19th Century. Neil hailed from Metarie and studied pre-med. Zach and Neil were both juniors at Tulane.

"How are things in Big D?" inquired Neil when Zach walked in.

"Had a good visit with the folks, but I was ready to get back. What time do we work out this afternoon?"

"Three o'clock, as usual. Coach Wells will run us pretty good. Need to get rid of some of that turkey and dressing."

Coach Cliff Wells was the Tulane University head basketball coach. The players both respected and liked him—not an easy accomplishment for any coach. Wells had built the '46 -'47 team with youngsters too young for the draft and a handful of returning war veterans. It proved a curious mixture. The vets barely tolerated the "young'uns", and the younger players resented the veterans coming back and taking their positions on the team. Coach Wells had a tough balancing act.

Zach looked at his watch. 2:45 p.m. He better get over to the gym, or coach would scratch him bald headed. Coach Wells was a strict and demanding disciplinarian. Zach had to get in line and shape up. The thought of Marie rose up from his memory bank. They played LSU on Friday night. He would call her after practice.

Zach slid into his sweats and hit the floor at 2:49 p.m. Coach cast a glance his way. "Hey. Tex, you cut it a little close."

Zach got the message and joined his teammates in a loosely organized shoot around. Zach's best shot was a 10-foot jumper. He also shot well from 18 feet and had a nice relaxed one-handed set shot. Nobody on the team could dunk the ball. White men can't jump. They began to run a figure eight warm-up drill that ended with a crip shot. Zach missed his first attempt.

"Nice shot, Ace," quipped a jesting roomy.

Practice consisted of the usual one-on-one drills and a 30-minute full court scrimmage. Zach was sucking air, but he gutted it out.

"Block out – block out," cried Coach Wells. "Meet the ball, Neil."

They ran wind sprints for another 10 minutes, and it was shower time. With grab-assing and towel popping out of the way, Zach and Neil walked back to the dorm. Coach had arranged for the dormitory kitchen to remain open, and the team settled in for some red beans and rice.

Zach seated himself at the one dormitory phone and dialed. Three rings.

"Hello."

Zach wasn't sure. He thought it was Marie. "May I speak with Marie, please?"

"This is Marie speaking."

Marie recognized Zach's measured easy drawl. "Is that you Zach?"

"You bet it is. You doing okay?"

"I was tired from the trip, but took a nap this afternoon, which helped a lot." Marie's voice sounded smooth and lyrical.

"Coach ran us good. I'm beat; but I called to ask you to come to the game Friday night." Zach felt a shot of adrenaline hit him. Would she, or would she not?

Marie responded, pleasantly. "I'd love it. What time does it start?"

"Eight o'clock. Could I pick you up?" Zach knew this would be a tight fit because he started suiting up at 6:30 p.m., and Marie probably wouldn't want to wait that long before the game. She took care of it, however.

"I'll have Martin drive me over for the game, and we can take the streetcar home after the game. I live only 10 blocks from the campus."

"Great, I'll meet you courtside after the game," said Zach with enthusiasm. "I'll leave a ticket for you at the Will Call window. Ask for it in my name."

"See you then," finished Marie in up tempo.

Friday afternoon finally rolled around. School was not in session because of the Christmas Break. Zach wondered about the crowd. They played LSU, so Zach expected a good house.

The Tulane band brought the Green Wave on the floor with

the fight song. The band looked small but sounded brassy and upbeat reflecting the ragtime New Orleans tradition. Zach loved the rush of excitement created by the band and cheerleaders. LSU was in deep trouble for this one.

Marie picked up her ticket at the Will Call window and found a seat on the wooden bleachers in the Tulane gym. She spotted Zach, immediately. Number 23. He looked good. Full shoulders filled out his warm-up gear. He had cast his warm-up pants aside earlier, revealing solid muscular legs. Actually, she thought him an excellent physical specimen. She had paid little attention to basketball or basketball players, preferring football as a game to watch. She had traveled to Baton Rouge on several occasions to watch LSU football.

Zach spotted her in the crowd. White starched shirt and brown skirt. Later he would notice brown penny loafers and bobby socks. She was, after all, a coed.

The warm up continued until a return to the dressing room.

"Boudreau, you and Jones start at guards. LaSalle and Jackson at forwards, and Braden at center. We'll start with a half-court press. Bother their guards, bringing the ball up. See if we can get some quick points off turnovers. Jackson, LaSalle, and Braden hit those boards. Let's go," said Coach Wells, attired in a natty hounds tooth double-breasted suit, complete with gray shirt and black tie. On his feet, he wore black wingtips.

The game was closely contested. Final score--Tulane 40, LSU 38. Zach hit one of his patented jumpers in the closing seconds for the win. His timing couldn't have been better. A host of well-wishing fans overcame him on the floor.

Neil wondered why Zach seemed so preoccupied after the game.

"Let's go get a burger," said Neil.

"Can't tonight, got a heavy date," replied Zach.

"With who, or whom?" Neil never felt confident about those objects of prepositions.

"Come on, I'll introduce you to her."

Neil seemed curious and followed Zach back out on the gym floor.

Marie waited, and Zach walked quickly up to her.

"Good game, Zach. It was fun."

"Thanks. Marie, this is Neil Jackson, my roomy."

Marie and Neil shook hands and nodded acquaintance.

"See y'all later," and Neil walked on to his date.

Marie and Zach stepped from the gym into the cold dampness of a New Orleans night. Tendrils of moisture arose from the bayous and river.

"Let's walk, if you are not too tired," announced Marie as she slid her arm into Zach's.

"Okay with me," responded Zach. Marie's presence would be worth a walk anywhere. Zach felt a growing attraction for her. Smelling a hint of perfume, he drew closer. She smelled sort of like fresh scrubbed lilac.

"I noticed you in the stands and had a hard time keeping my eye on the game."

"Really?"

"Your essence is nearly equal to your beauty. What is that perfume, Marie?"

"Whoa there cowboy, that's pretty strong stuff. Nearly poetic."

They turned their coat collars up. The mist became a light drizzle.

"Basketball is poetry in motion, just as dance is an art form."

"You speak pretty words, Zach. Maybe you are a poet and don't know it." toyed Marie.

"I doubt it. I do like to write. You know, mostly themes and the like. We just finished Beowulf and all that old English rhyme. Got Chaucer's *Canterbury Tales* coming up," said Zach.

"I have thought about writing," continued Marie, "That's one of the reasons I attend Loyola."

Marie and Zach walked along St. Charles Avenue where moss-covered century-old oak trees stood. Street lamps framed this sylvan beauty. Zach could hear a foghorn in the distance. A comfortable closeness began to grow between Marie and Zach; it sprang from understanding between them as well as emotional and physical chemistry.

"Here we are," said Marie and directed Zach through an iron gate flanked by an iron picket fence.

A few steps brought them to the front porch. Subdued light from cottage lanterns framed the door. Four huge Romanesque columns fronted the house, the biggest house Zach had ever seen up close and personal. Zach and Marie faced each other. He took both of her hands in his. Her brown hazel gaze shook him. He bent forward but a light touch of her hand on his lips intercepted him.

"Not tonight. You are sweet Zach," she tossed out nonchalantly.

Zach stepped back. "Can I see you tomorrow, and make a day of it in the *Vieux Carre?*"

"Your French is not too bad, and for that I am inclined to accept your offer."

"What time?" inquired Zach.

"Can you leave at 9 a.m.? If so, we can catch the streetcar down to Canal and walk on over to Cafe du Monde for beignets and café au lait."

"You will see me at 8:55 a.m." and after a kiss to her raised hand, he retreated down the cobblestone walkway, raised the latch on the heavy iron gate, passed through, and carefully shut the gate behind him.

The moon waned slowly in the cool mist and mellow fruitfulness of a fog-shrouded New Orleans night. A light drizzle had turned to rain. However, he was in luck, catching a streetcar not far from Marie's house. A few blocks over, a fellow worked on a story about another streetcar in New Orleans. *Stella!*

Chapter 6
▼▼▼

"Marie, who was that young man at the door with you tonight"? questioned her mother, the Baroness Julie Calve Tranchepaine.

"His name's Zach LaSalle," responded Marie with a lilt in her voice.

The Baroness came into Marie's room, positioned a cigarette in a holder and curled it into 50-year-old lips, exaggerated with smudged-on lipstick.

"Did you say LaSalle? Mmm, a fine French name. Is his family native New Orleans?" she asked with a sense of *haute* inquisitiveness.

Marie grew irritated from the line of questioning, but she expected it from her mother who along with the Baron had adopted her as their own when she was a tiny infant.

"No, he is not from New Orleans. He is from Dallas, Texas and is a student at Tulane. As far as I can determine, he is a very nice solid young man," Marie said reassuringly. "Not everybody with the name of LaSalle can be from New Orleans."

Madame Baroness Julia poured herself a Scotch on the rocks as was her evening habit. Her arched brow furrowed, "Is he a lad of ordinary means?"

"Ordinary in what sense, *Mere*?"

"You know what I mean. Does he have resources?"

"I only recently met him, and I haven't quizzed him about his pecuniary status," Marie spurted out, sarcastically.

"*Soit!*" Madam Tranchepaine exited Marie's bedroom in a haze of cigarette smoke. She leaned back in. "By the way, your father will arrive tomorrow. He and Governor Davis have been duck hunting. I am certain he will want to know about young Lafayette."

"LaSalle, Mother, LaSalle."

Mysterious love, uncertain treasure;
Hast thou more of pain or pleasure!
Endless torments dwell about thee;
Yet who would love and live without thee!
--Addison – Rosamond. Act III. Sc. 2.

Chapter 7
▼▼▼

The door latch sounded Zach's arrival at Maria's home the next morning.

"It is 8:55 a.m. You are a man of your word," called Marie, before she dashed off into another room. "Come in, and have a seat. I'll be ready in a minute."

Zach had observed the mansion as he walked along St. Charles Avenue on several occasions, but had never had the opportunity to come inside before. A row of rhododendrons backed by azaleas framed the front porch of this three-story French colonial. Marie had told him the home had been in the Tranchepaine family for over a hundred years. Baron Tranchepaine was fourth generation aristocratic French Creole. He had inherited his fortune from early Tranchepaine successes in sugarcane farming and various import businesses.

Zach assumed the room he stood in served as a parlor. It had a black and white marble floor arranged in a diamond design. Zach didn't know it, but he had taken a seat on an American Empire sofa. Black horsehair fabric encased the mahogany furniture. Green silk damask drapes with gold bullion fringe adorned the windows. A gondola chair stood paired with a mahogany center table covered in a matching green silk damask tablecloth. The buff wallpaper with *trompe le frieze* and panel molding finished out the décor. Family pictures hung in precision around the room; and a bronzed Rodin sculpture of "The Kiss" sat in a glass case on one wall.

    Marie returned. She thought Zach looked impressive seated on the sofa.

    "This is a beautiful house, Marie."

    "Would you like to see more?" she inquired.

    "If you don't mind, I surely would." Eagerness crept into Zach's voice.

    "This is a typical French Colonial house, Zach. Those are original coral colored bricks on the outside. Of course, all colonials have dormers."

    "That's what I am," interjected Zach. "I live in a dorm just up the road." Quips came readily to Zach's lips.

    "Bad, really bad," continued Marie, looking impatient. "Do you even care what a dormer is? How about the fact that the four columns outside are topped with gabled ends forming pediments. Pay attention to detail. That's what makes life interesting."

    "If you say so Marie, but I think this is out of my league. Keep going, though, you've got my attention."

    "Come, let me show you the sitting room."

    He followed her down a wide hallway.

    "This is where I read and study."

    Empire style bookcases lined the walls. "I do some needlework here, too." She lovingly stroked a gilt-decorated sewing stand, then turned to him. "We better get going." She picked a parasol from a rack and allowed Zach to follow her out the door.

The morning felt cool and invigorating. A damp wind blew off Lake Ponchatrain. Marie and Zach boarded the streetcar and headed toward Canal Street.

Zach could smell her perfume, again. It seemed to capture Marie's essence. The scent captivated him. They sat opposite a couple smooching and cooing like lovesick doves. Zach reached for Marie's hand. She obliged. The warmth and softness of her skin gave Zach a little stir.

The swaying streetcar ran parallel to the Mississippi River. St. Charles Avenue made a long concave curve as it intersected with Canal Street. Hence, the moniker of Crescent City. Marie and Zach stepped from the streetcar onto Canal Street, the widest street in America, originally designed to carry water in a long canal. It never happened.

"Let's try Chartres Street. I love the antique shops along the way," Marie said, taking the lead.

Zach had visited the French Quarter many times, and found a certain uniqueness about it that prohibited ennui. On this special occasion, he looked at this place – a site chosen by Iberville in 1718 – through Marie's eyes. Ironically, the most indelible impression left by the Spanish was the Spanish architecture found in the "French Quarter." French and Caribbean touches gave it added depth.

At the turn of the 19th century, many whites and free men of colour came from the French colony of Saint Dominique. They were artisans, craftsmen and sculptors who played a prominent role in building the houses, balconies and monuments in the *Vieux Carre*.

The iron lace work of the balconies, the heavy iron doors and bolts and gratings came from Spain.

Marie and Zach walked along Chartres, hand-in-hand, to the pleasant sound of fountains bubbling behind enclosed walls with arcades and *les cours* (courtyards). They passed Napoleon's House.

Zach raised the question with Marie. "Did Napoleon ever live in that house?"

"No, but he had the opportunity when they exiled him. Quite a commotion took place getting the house ready for him", Marie replied.

They continued to stroll down Chartres. Marie removed a light jacket, revealing a red blouse underneath, which she wore with a fitted black skirt and black shoes. She cut a striking, womanly figure, and Zach took pleasure in the fact that she held onto his arm.

"Would you come with me to the Cathedral?" Marie asked.

"Sure. Lead the way."

Marie and Zach entered St. Louis Cathedral, and Marie bowed and *genoux se mettre*'d. Since Zach was Methodist, he was used to kneeling only for communion. He stood silent as Marie worshiped. After arising, she and Zach left the oldest continually active cathedral in the United States.

They left the Cathedral known as the heart of the *Vieux Carre*. They walked along the *Place de Arms*. "The Baroness Pontalba had these fences installed and landscaped this route many years ago," said Marie.

"Baroness Pontalaba," joined Zach.

"No Pontalba. She also had all of the apartments along here built. Quite a lady."

Zach realized Marie's attention to detail had surfaced again.

"What else do you know about this area?" asked Zach.

"Look up there, Zach, see those initials A and P. They represent the maiden and married name of Baroness Pontalba."

As they walked, Marie remarked that she "just loved the banana and myrtle trees inside Jackson Square."

Zach noticed them for the first time, making him further aware of Marie's uncanny eye for things. She responded sensitively to her surroundings, and was quite knowledgeable about New Orleans.

They walked into the open space of *Café du Mond*, and a waiter quickly seated them on round stool chairs with metal backs.

Zach ordered, after first seeking Marie's desire. "We'll have a plate of *beignets* and two *café au lait*, please."

Marie smiled in amusement and looked lovingly at Zach. "Zach it's 'caffy-oh-lay.' Not 'cafaa ah lay it.'"

For a man with a French name, Zach wasn't much of a Frenchman. He grinned sheepishly, and said, "I'm a good learner, and you can teach me anytime." He leaned forward and planted a soft kiss on Marie's cheek.

When he drew away, he realized Marie's face looked slightly flushed. She dropped her gaze.

"*Café au lait* is chicory coffee served with steaming milk. Black and white", Marie explained as she slowly stirred her coffee.

Zach handed Marie the plate of *beignets*. She daintily lifted one of the square donuts with an exquisite hand and dropped it onto her saucer. After the first bite, a small amount of powdered sugar remained on her upper lip, which was as full and desirable as her lower one.

"Can I help get that sugar off your lips?" Zach inquired, hoping he wasn't coming on too strong.

"Later, if it's still there," teased Marie.

People come up to me and they ask me, are you going to play your 'Tin Roof Blues'? ... I play it like I always play it. ...But you know no music is my music. It's everybody's who can feel it. If you can feel it--then it's yours too. You got to be in the sun to feel the sun. It's the way with music, too.
--Sidney Bechet. *Treat it Gentle.* 1960. Bethany Bultman, New Orleans Fodor's Publication, 1996.

The Red Dog Oyster Club sits nestled off Bourbon Street. It's late and money is tight and so are the patrons.— A hard rain beats down on a tin roof. It is *The Tin Roof Blues.*

Chapter 8
▼▼▼

Zach and Marie savored their donuts and coffee.

Marie casually studied Zach. He had a good face—somewhat chiseled and Romanesque. His soft blue eyes were penetrating, searching, and he held his head high. He had a square jaw and full lips. He wore his brown hair short and neatly combed. Though broad, his hands felt soft to the touch, not clammy.

The sun began to penetrate a light fog, which had draped the city since dawn.

"Would you like a moon walk?" inquired Marie.

"That would take us a little far, wouldn't it?"

"Not a moon up there," Marie rolled her eyes upward, "but over there."

Zach had strolled along the old military walkway before; however, he didn't know it had another name—"moonwalk".

He and Marie took a good look at the Mississippi River and the boats plying its waters. Freighters, barges and tug boats dominated the scene. They strolled arm in arm and talked about the incredible history of the place.

French explorers had once traversed this river. The British had started up the river in 1699 in the English corvette, *Carolina Galley*. The *Galley* had carried prospective settlers, and sailed approximately 75 miles up river from the Gulf. Bienville left a French fort at Biloxi and explored the Mississippi River with a small *coterie* of Frenchmen. He encountered the British, and a British officer asked for the location of the Mississippi River. Bienville told him the river lay further west and, furthermore, he stood in French territory heavily guarded by forts. If he proceeded further up the river, he would face great danger. The bluff worked. The British vessel weighed anchor, turned around and sailed toward the Gulf.

The point 10 miles below New Orleans where the encounter took place was named English Turn after the encounter. Had the British not met Bienville, they might have succeeded in colonizing New Orleans before the French and Spanish. A century later, not far from English Turn, the Battle of New Orleans was fought, and once again the British were rebuffed.

French Acadians (Cajuns) came down the river from Canada. Indians preceded everybody coming into Southern Louisiana. John Law, an Impresario Scotsman, hustled French aristocrats to invest in the Nouveau Orleans; and he arranged for the poor and downtrodden of Europe to come and work the fields for the French investors.

In the early 18th Century, Germans came from the Rhine region, later to become consummate farmers in the area. Villars Dubriel, a German, became a contractor for the Mississippi Valley and, not far from where Marie and Zach stood, built the first levee in New Orleans.

In 1729 the French Company of the West began the flood of slaves into the area. The company governed slavery conditions. The location where slaves arrived later grew to be known as Congo Square. Strains of New Orleans jazz began to emerge along the waterfront.

"New Orleans has always been French," Marie said wistfully as she leaned forward on a railing and peered out over the Mississippi River. "Even during the Spanish domination, the people here spoke French. French colonials brought their families into the region, and all other peoples were assimilated one way or the other with French culture. I am a French Creole, Zach, like you are a French Texan."

"I have never understood exactly what the word Creole represented," commented Zach.

Marie replied, "The word 'Creole' is derived from the Spanish *criollo,* which means a child born in the colonies. Therefore native-born French, Spanish or persons of colour are considered 'Creole'."

"My mother is Scotch/Irish," Zach announced with certainty.

"Ah the Irish, this river is full of past secrets. In the early 1800's the rowdy, hot-tempered, whiskey-drinking Irish came down the river. They were the first 'Americans' and not liked very well. The 'Kaintucks' were keel boatmen bringing whiskey, flour, coffee, soap, and textiles down the river. Kentucky and Tennessee were both home to these folks. Add rice, indigo, sugar, tobacco and cotton, which is home grown, and you have the beginning elements of New Orleans as a great port city. Also Yankee businessmen and southern planters with names like Smith and Miller began to show up."

"Marie, you sound just like my history professor."

"You have to know your history and where you come from, Zach, in order to know yourself. New Orleans is a big melting pot, but stirred mostly by Creole and Cajun cooking."

Zach liked Marie's thoughtful and pretty words. "If you write like you talk, you will make a wonderful writer some day."

I have been playing that horn since 1894 on steamboats, in Honky Tonks and in parades.
--Bunk Johnson

Watch your step for we are boarding the old sternwheeler Fate Marable and are bound for New Orleans. Mark Twain is at the helm and greets his passengers with this bit of wisdom:

> *So far it has been a mighty good day and it is going to get better as we listen to some music for the ages. It is honest and happy music. Leave your irritations and meanness behind and think grace and beauty of New Orleans jazz. A music that drifts like leaves on the surface of the mind, and then sinks deep into the soul. Do you hear the lap lap of the river and soft tinkling of the ivories, and perhaps a distant banjo? Up with the gang plank, cast off the bowline, roll the wheel, it's full steam ahead as we go a floatin' down the ole green Mississippi River.*

Chapter 9
▼▼▼

The noon sun penetrated the clouds, and although low in the sky, provided warmth to the humid air along the river. Zach and Marie strolled leisurely on the cobblestone moonwalk and again entered Jackson Square. A street artist, with pallet in hand, studiously eyed his subject. Marie and Zach paused momentarily to watch. He sketched with what looked like large chalky crayons. Zach thought about asking him to paint a portrait of Marie, but an equally challenging thought about his finances dampened his enthusiasm.

Shops and eateries surrounding Jackson Square had opened for business. Proprietors busily swept up the previous night's debris. A faint hint of beer emanated from Cappuccino's Bar. Zach looked in over low swinging doors and observed patrons seated at the bar; a world unfamiliar to him. The clip clop clattering of horse hoofs alerted Zach to move Marie and himself further away from a tourist carriage passing by.

"Why don't we go over to the Market Place?" suggested Marie.

"Fine with me. Where is it?"

"A couple of blocks over. The Market Place is the center of

New Orleans, and early on, furnished the staples for the culinary appetites of the city."

"Everything is so hot and saucy. Keeps my nose running."

"It's good for you, Zach. Makes your blood run hot."

"I'll bet you're one of those hot-blooded French Creole ladies," said Zach as he put his arm tightly around Marie's petite waist.

"Do you know anything about herbs?" inquired Marie.

"Only Herb Jones, our second string guard," deadpanned Zach.

Marie smiled. She had grown used to Zach's off the wall dry wit.

"The Ursuline sisters introduced herbs to the area."

"Aren't they an act in the Quarter?"

Marie paid no attention. "Look here Zach, these bay leaves are for stews; this dill will help you sleep; parsley for looks; oregano to help relieve a full stomach; garlic and sage for seasoning; and shallots for strength. Here is some old time sagamite. Mix this with ground corn and butter, and you have grits. You like grits?"

"Only with sausage, eggs and biscuits," grinned Zach. "How come you know so much about cooking?"

"French ladies know about cooking, even though some never have to cook. It is tradition. I can cook the gumbos and stews with the best of them. I'll cook you some Lentil Creole soup sometime.

We have to give credit to the Spanish, however, for the tomatoes and peppers. Mix up some *court bouillon*; add a little garlic and artichoke, and *voila,* you have Jambalaya."

"We had a guy on our team named Arty who never could hit a free throw. We called him 'artychoke'." Zach laughed, but Marie did not.

All the talk about food had made them hungry, and they

headed for the Royale Café on St. Peter Street. Along the way, Zach noticed that a pigeon had left his calling card on the shoulder of General Jackson. It appeared that nature had little respect for history.

They slid into seats in the Café Royale glad to get off their feet for a while.

"Hello, I am Pierre Cordelet. May I help you?" He handed them both menus, then dried his hands on a stained white apron.

After a few minutes of cogitation, Marie and Zach were ready to order. Zach raised his hand and motioned to Pierre.

"Bring us some of this 'cort bullun'," Zach announced, proudly.

"He means coo-bo-yon."

Zach stood corrected, again.

Marie smiled, "You'll eventually get the hang of it."

"You're a marvel, Marie."

A few minutes later, the waiter placed a brimming super bowl of fish stew in front of Zach and Marie. Pierre beamed, "anchovies, lobster, crab, Creole mustard, red sauce and rice. Enjoy!"

"We'll also have two caffy-oh-lay's," said Zach with emphasis on the last two syllables.

Marie nodded an appreciative glance.

They had walked for more than five hours. Time and closeness begets intimacy. In close proximity, personal chemistries either blend or separate.

Marie thought that Zach "wore well." She leaned forward after taking a lingering sip of coffee. "Do you have plans for the future?"

"I haven't thought too much about it. I like athletics and might end up coaching. If I could, I would like to play my trumpet here in New Orleans."

"There is more to life than jazz and basketball. Have you considered studying to become a doctor, lawyer, businessman or even a college professor?"

Watching Marie, Zach realized she had advanced further in her plans than he. His most immediate plan had to do with tasting those ruby red lips nestled in that pretty face of hers.

"I've got to declare a major next semester. Don't know yet. I kind of like psychology and sociology."

" What can you do with those majors? You need balance. It's good to know things, but it also is good to learn to do something. The life of the mind is important, but so is the pocketbook." Marie shrugged her shoulders and let the matter go.

Zach thought about his pocketbook and how it had grown increasingly thinner as the day wore along. His finances consisted of room, board, books, tuition and 20 bucks a month spending money athletic scholarship at Tulane.

They lingered in Café Royale and munched on pralines. Zach could hear the faint melodic sounds of Dixieland Jazz drifting in from outside. He grew restless. "Are you ready to go?"

"Let me take a trip to the ladies room, and then we may go." Marie excused herself, and Zach took the opportunity to make a visit himself. Inside, he noticed somebody had left him messages on the wall.

Zach paid the bill; Pierre inherited a two-bit tip, and they meandered out onto the street again. The jazz flowed strong from close by as they walked on down St. Peter Street. The doors of Preservation Jazz Hall stood open on this late Saturday afternoon.

"Do you like Dixieland Jazz?" asked Zach.

"I like New Orleans Dixieland Jazz." responded Marie.

In they went, arm in arm, to Preservation Hall.

The Kid Ory Jazz Band winged its way on Storyville Blues, a slow ad-lib drag. Kid Ory, the dean of the New Orleans tailgate trombone style, provided long, glistening punctuation for the phrases played by Andy Blakeney's trumpet. Guitarist Johnny St. Cyr clunked out a steady rhythmic beat. Bob McCracken's clarinet played solo above the fray. Bob Van Eps' piano gave a ragged edge to the matter. Bob Boyack pumped the bass fiddle, and Doc Cenardo backed it all up with a steady boom, boom, boom, boom.

An elegant lady in a tight fitting gown stood in front of the band, and with a strong bravado voice, began to sing:

> *I'm an old time queen, from New Orleans,*
> *who lived in Storyille.*
> *As I sang the blues, and tried to amuse,*
> *that's how I paid my bills.*
> *Well the law steps in, he called it sin,*
> *just to have a little fun,*
> *and the police stopped by, and made us stop.*
> *And Storyville is done.*
> *Now get on a steamboat, or go get yourself a train,*
> *I mean a slow old train.*
> *They made me move out, and I never got back.*
> *Go get your ticket, because thay's no more drag.*

The band moved into the final ensemble, and the lady did an easy swaying of the hips, with a little fun loving shimmy that mesmerized the small crowd made of jazz mavens and touriists.' You could tell the difference. The mavens' faces lit up, and their bodies gently swayed. The naivetes clapped on the downbeat.

Zach thought he had died and gone to heaven. He could not understand why this music moved him this way. He figured it worked something like sunlight – once it shines on you long enough it changes the color of your skin. With enough exposure, the effect becomes permanent.

The band took a break.

"Hello, Honey, and who is this young man checking me out?" inquired the singing lady in the aqua colored dress.

"This is Zach LaSalle, Mama. Zach, this is my mother, Kate Robicheaux."

Zach looked at Marie and could tell she was completely serious. He stood, speechless. He mumbled, incoherently, but managed to offer his hand in salutation to Marie's "Mother!" His mind continued to whir. If this was Marie's mother, then who was the lady in the house on St. Charles Avenue? How many "mothers" did Marie have? A thousand questions inundated his mind.

Marie grinned and looked at Zach, who in turn also had a sheepish grin. "How's that for a rim shot, Zach?"

While Zach recovered from meeting "Mom," the Kid Ory band returned and took their seats on rounded wooden chairs. They all wore white long sleeved shirts and ties. They had obviously shed their coats to their three-piece suits. They kept their vests on.

"Miss Marie, would you like to do a number?" Kid Ory asked in a gracious and formal manner.

Marie hesitated.

"Ah go on baby. We'd love it," urged Mama Kate.

"Okay, okay." Marie centered herself in front of the band. They had no microphone. "How about 'Sister Kate'?" she inquired of the band.

The Kid nodded approval, and stomped his foot - one, two; one, two, three, four, and the band bit into "I Wish I Could Shimmy Like My Sister Kate." They initiated a couple of introductory bars then softened their tone. Marie slightly raised her head and began:

> *Oh boy, wish I could shimmy like my 'Mama' Kate,*
>   blowing a kiss to Kate, now seated with Zach,
> *She could shake it like jelly on a plate.*
> *My Mama made quite a sight,*
> *While she danced most of the night.*
> *Every man in the neighborhood,*
> *Knew she could shimmy ever so good.*
> *I'll never be late with my date,*
>   With a teasing finger motioned toward Zach,
> *When I can shimmy like my Mama Kate,*
> *I'm shoutin,'*
> *Shimmy like my Mama Kate, Oh boy.*

Andy Blakeney's trumpet took the lead, followed by the Kid's long, slurred, wailing trombone. Marie sent a chill through Zach as she started a little shimmy moving her hips back and forth, to and fro; and with hands raised and a body-shakin' motion, she brought it on home, accompanied by the Kid and his sidekicks.

> *No, I'll never be late with Zach as my date,*
> *When I can shimmy like my Mama, Kate,*
> *I'm shoutin',*
> *Shimmy like my sister; no I mean shimmy like my Mama, Kate.*

Zach felt stunned and enraptured at the same time, and the

small crowd clapped their appreciation.

Kate and Zach made room for Marie as she joined them at a small table.

"The shake never falls far from the bake, child; you're gettin' better than ever." Kate glowed her appreciation.

Kid Ory announced the next number. "Here is a oldie written by King Oliver in the 20's. 'Dr. Jazz.'"

The band began a clean and pure rendition in the traditional New Orleans manner. After an opening ensemble and riffs by Bob McCracken on clarinet and Bob Eps on piano, trumpeter Andy Blakeney stepped forward.

Hello Central, give me Dr. Jazz,
He's got what I need, I'll say he has,
Cause when the world goes wrong,
And I've got the blues,
He's the man makes me put on my dancin' shoes.
The more I get, the more I want it seems,
All I see is Dr. Jazz in my dreams.
With all the problems I seem to have,
Hello Central, give me Dr. Jazz.

The streets of the *Vieux Carre* edged toward darkness. Jazz enthusiasts who appreciated the power and artistic beauty of the truly American art form filled what precious space there was left in the Preservation Hall.

Zach felt elated by the musical knot beginning to form between him and Marie; and he could tell that her new Mama was a special person.

"I'm going to have to leave, kids. Mama gotta keep movin'. You take care of Marie, you hear. Bye now." Kate waved to the band members and left.

Zach's glance followed her through the door. A man in fancy duds opened the car for Kate. She got in, and they drove off in a long white Packard sedan.

Edward "Kid" Ory grew up a Creole of colour on the San Francisco Plantation upriver from New Orleans. As a teenager, he led a "spasm" or "gutbucket" band in Storyville, Lincoln Park and at the New Orleans Country Club. He played with all the greats–King Oliver, Louis Armstrong, Jelly Roll Morton, and Sidney Bechet. Edward Ory announced the next number.

"Ole Jelly Roll himself wrote this next one, 'Milneberg Joys,' a stomp rag about life up around Lake Ponchatrain at the Milneberg Dance Hall."

The band rode with merriment and excitement into the number. It became hard to talk over the blaring horns, but Zach couldn't get Kate off his mind. "Marie, I'm confused," he said over the din of music. "Tell me about the 'Mom' I just met."

"She and my Dad were lovers. As a quadroon lady, she lived in an apartment on Rampart Street. She was more than his *placee*. She was his love. She is my blood mother."

It grew hard to talk over the roar of "Milneberg Joys," but Marie continued. "I'm a 'love child' of the Quarter. My father married the Baroness, not knowing of my conception. The Baron and Kate fought over me, and you see who prevailed. My father and mother adopted me six months after my birth. It nearly killed Mama Kate. Father doesn't think Mama Julia knows – that only he, Mama Kate and I know. I am sure Julia knows, but we never discuss it. Both my Mamas love me, and that is what matters. I am an Octoroon *Café au lait*, Zach; one eighth chicory, and seven eighths milk. No use peeling the grape any further, that's it."

Zach sat back in his chair, then leaned forward and took Marie's hand and kissed it. The Kid Ory band finished another set with the Winin' Boy Blues. Marie blew a kiss to the band members and she and Zach prepared to leave.

Chapter 10
▼▼▼

Once back on St. Peter Street, Zach and Marie headed for Bourbon Street. The night air felt chilly and damp, portending of rain. Marie put on her khaki coat and pulled the collar up, and Zach did the same with his jacket. A purple haze punctuated by blinking neon lights encased Bourbon Street.

Spielers hustled patrons for the strip joints. Seah Moore and her 45's graced one marquee. Zach took a furtive glance. No luck, you had to pay to see. Young kids of colour danced with clattering steel taps, keeping their own rhythm. A lone soloist played a mournful tune on a bass clarinet. Hedonism prevailed, and the street came alive with lookers and a few hookers that spilled over from Perdido, Basin and Rampart Streets.

The Famous Door, opened in 1932, was Zach's favorite place. A picture of Bunk Johnson and his New Orleans Band hung in a glass enclosed case on the outside wooden wall.

"Just a minute, Marie." Zach came to a halt. He could hear

Bunk's band cooking to "That's a Plenty." Too late today, but Zach knew he had to come back next Saturday. "You and me and Bunk Johnson a week from tonight. Agreed?"

"Agreed," responded Marie.

They moved on to the vanishing sound of Bunk's band.

Zach turned to Marie as they cleared Bourbon Street and made their way up Canal to the St. Charles streetcar. "Jazz is a lot like basketball," Zach said. "You play together as a team with each person making a particular contribution. The game and song may be the same, and it is never played the same way twice. The imagination can soar, but it is disciplined with technique. You have to be both abstract and concrete to play jazz and basketball. Jazz is really high math with preciseness and clarity as a virtue. Dixieland 'Jass', as it was originally called, consists of leftover horns from Civil war days; church music; African rhythm; marching bands; two-four, four-four beats; and syncopation.

It is cakewalkin', struttin', ragtime, gutbucket, stompin', Vaudeville, burlesque pit bands, paddle wheelers, Tin Pan Alley, Roarin' 20's Speakeasies and American, French, and British high society ladies in slinky dresses and jeweled headbands."

"Whew, Zach LaSalle, where did that come from?" asked a quizzical Marie.

"It's a soul thing, and what I just said is the only way I know to describe it. There is a virtuous beauty to it."

"You think you are a philosopher?"

"Prof Duflot says that Philo means to search, and Sophia means wisdom. So anyone seeking truth and wisdom is a philosopher. Authentic New Orleans jazz truthfully moves the spirit. You can't make up truth, Marie. You encounter it."

He could tell his speech had impressed Marie.

"Come on Zach, we better hurry if we plan to catch the next streetcar."

Rain spattered down as they boarded the car, shook off the wetness and settled into one of many vacant seats.

Away from the cacophony of Bourbon Street, the quiet ride on the streetcar came as a welcome relief. They made the short walk to the Elegante de Arms, easily.

Zach had learned in life that if you don't expect much, life rarely disappoints you. However, he found he couldn't control his expectations as he moved through the gate toward Marie's front porch. The porch lights provided enough light for Zach to look deeply into Marie's eyes, which told him, yes? Or no?

She answered the question moving toward Zach and reaching for his shoulders with willing arms. She stood 5'8", willowy and fleshy. At 6'3" Zach had to bend forward, slightly. Their bodies closed together and made a good fit. Zach's lips moved to her cheek and neck. Slowly she turned and caught him flush on the lips.

Marie appeared to have wanted this moment as much as Zach. Her lips felt full, soft and slightly parted. The kiss became passionate, and Marie's body shuddered lightly. Their lips parted but their bodies grew closer. The next kiss turned deep and full, unlike anything Zach had ever experienced. He became engulfed by a full mouth which seared his senses and body like a bolt of lightning.

Marie and Zach parted and caught breaths from the explosiveness of their contact.

"Maybe we better sit down, Zach," said Marie softly as she beckoned him to join her on the porch swing.

Zach slowly regained his senses and sat down beside Marie.

They moved the swing gently back and forth, not talking.

"Zach, would you like to have Sunday dinner with the Tranchepaines? We will attend Early Mass and sit for dinner at 12:30. Can you make it?"

"Does a coon dog have fleas? You know I'll come."

"Good, the Baron and Baroness will want to meet you."

With that settled, Zach gently kissed Marie's hand and held it close and lingering to his lips. They arose from the swing, and Zach followed her to the door.

"Good night, Zach."

"Good night, Marie."

Zach walked back to the campus. He had thought about trying to get his old blue pickup from Dallas over to New Orleans, but wasn't sure it would make the trip. He sure could use it, but Marie probably wouldn't be too impressed.

Back in the dorm, he joined a late night poker game. Gambling was against the rules. But the stakes ran pretty low as they only used matches. Pinky had just won a big pot with three fours.

"Man, where you been all day?" asked Glynn Braden.

"Probably in the Quarter," imparted Pinky.

Zach just smiled. There was no way they could have a clue as to how delicious his day had been. *Beignets, café' au lait,* Dixieland Jazz, Marie's "other Mom," and Marie. How *merveilleux* and *tu es superbe!* He knew a little French. And speaking of French, did he get French kissed, or did he get French kissed?

Alas! The love of women! It is known to be a lovely and fearful thing.
--Bryon, Don Juan. Canton II.

Chapter 11
▼▼▼

School was back in session, and Zach enjoyed the delight of a solid breakfast of bacon and eggs in the athletic dorm. On this Sunday morning, he decided to wear his one dark suit for dinner with Marie. He might as well go to the little Methodist church close by. This Sunday morning had dawned clear and crisp, unusual for a January day in New Orleans.

He entered the Methodist church and took a seat in the rear of the sanctuary. After a hymn, he stood with the congregation.

I believe in God the Father Almighty,
Maker of heaven and earth;
And in Jesus Christ, His only Son our Lord;
Who was conceived by the Holy Spirit,
Born of the Virgin Mary, suffered under Pontius Pilate,
Was crucified, dead and buried
… … …
I believe in the Holy Spirit, the Holy atholic church.

Zach paused in the recitation. He had always wondered how Methodists could believe in the Catholic church, until someone explained to him that catholic meant universal.

Zach's family had raised him in the Methodist Church. His father worked as a high school football coach and his mother was a high school Latin teacher in Dallas. He had grown up a product of oxymoronish hell-raising/puritanical Texas. He had the Texan's spirit of adventure cloaked with civility and restraint. Experience had taught him to achieve and demonstrate whatever talent he might possess; that caring for others was more important than one's own self-absorption.

Zach's ancestral memory bank prized love as the highest virtue, followed by a sense of justice and fair play. Peace and civility should win out over violence and conflict. Compassion, tolerance and forgiveness weighed superior to condemnation and retribution.

His family also taught him that it was better to give than take; to keep his self-esteem in balance by cultivating a sense of humility and humor; to shrink his ego, and expand his soul; and to seek grace and beauty in human lives and the world around him.

His parents also taught him not to go "all the way" with young ladies until married. However, it had come to him only recently that if he thought this through, he might also request forgiveness and receive it after the fact for this "sin", should it ever trip him up.

Contemplating this in some depth, to his dismay, he realized while he might be the foreplay king of Dallas at the moment, that was it—thus far.

Play and after play crept into Zach's mind when he thought of Marie. He wanted to see her again. He found her intriguing.

He arrived at the residence of Baron Antoinne and Baroness Julie Calve Tranchepaine at 12:15 and knocked on the door. A lady of colour in starched white linen with a chignon headdress greeted him. "Are you Zach LaSalle?"

Zach nodded.

"Please come in. The Trachepaines are expecting you. I am Liz Maelson." She extended her hand, which Zach shook politely.

Marie joined him momentarily, radiant and smiling. The two gently embraced.

Zach looked appealing, thought Marie, in his dark blue suit, white starched shirt, and red tie neatly pulled up tight in a Windsor knot.

Marie looked good in anything, but today she wore a tight fitting black dress with hose and high heels. A small red rose accented her neatly pulled back black hair.

Baron Tranchepaine entered the room, nattily attired in a gray business suit.

Zach moved to meet him. "I am Zach LaSalle."

"Marie has told me about you. I an Antoinne Tranchepaine. Tony might be easier to remember. Please keep your seat."

The trio became a quartet as Julia joined Zach, Marie and Tony.

After the introductions, Julia beckoned to Liz who stood on the fringe of the parlor. "Would you please bring us all a mint julep?"

Zach thought – a mint julep, in January? However, he didn't voice the question, and enjoyed the julep when it came as well as the polite conversation that followed.

Martin, whom Zach remembered from the day he picked Marie up at the train station, appeared in the parlor doorway. "Dinner is served."

Julia led the group into the formal dining room, located in

the center of the first floor. Jasmine candles scented the room. A dimly lit, gilt bronze Louis XIV style chandelier highlighted the room. The chandelier hung precipitously low over the table.

Zach observed that the walls were tinted a sandalwood brown, and massive black doors led out onto a gallery, complementing dark wooden wainscoting.

The long mahogany dining room table was set with Old Paris china and Bohemian amber glass etched with animals in a forest scene. Straight-legged mahogany chairs complemented the table. The floor looked like a massive brown and tan checker set.

An 18th Century carved gilt-edged Italian mirror hung over the fireplace.

Julia and Tony took their seats at each end of the table with Zach and Marie situated across from one another in the middle. Zach thought, with amazement, that at least they were within shouting distance.

The salads were served.

The Baron said, "Marie tells me you are a basketball player at Tulane. I noticed in the *Times-Picayune* that you have beaten LSU and Georgia Tech. That's a good start."

"Zach scored the winning basket, Daddy," added Marie with further embellishment. "He is really quite a good player."

"Tulane is an outstanding university. It had the first School of Commerce in the country. I studied at Tulane, but we wanted Marie to go Loyola where her mother went."

Tony inquired, "What are you studying, Zach?"

Zach was better prepared to answer the question than when Marie had posed it to him earlier. "Right now I am leaning toward coaching."

"Coaching, why would you want to coach? No money in

that. Are you taking any business courses?"

"Not yet," replied Zach, knowing full well that he probably never would because business and finance were of no interest to him.

"Tulane has excellent law and medical schools. You might think about that," retorted Tony as he moved back slightly for Liz to remove his salad plate.

"Marie said you just got back from duck hunting and had a quacking good time." Zach wished he hadn't said that, but as Alice said in "The Looking Glass," "Once you've said it, you can't take it back."

Julia laughed out loud. Tony was not amused, and Marie held her head low and grinned.

"Hunting was good. Do you hunt?" inquired Tony.

"Not much. Back in Texas, we hunt mostly dove, quail and deer. When I was a kid, I used to go out and shoot jackrabbits. I'm not too fond of guns."

"Guns are a necessity. I wouldn't be without one. I'll show you my collection. You might change your mind after you've seen it. Some have been in the family for years."

The salad plates had been cleared, and Liz placed a meal of shrimp in a tart remoulade sauce, au gratin vegetables, and creamed spinach before the eating quartet. A large basket of baguettes and *brioches,* which had been picked up at La Madeleine by Martin, were placed in the middle of the table.

Martin had entered with a bottle of white wine. Tony sniffed the cork. "Very good, Martin."

Martin poured the wine.

Tony, Julia and Marie raised their glasses.

"To Zach, Marie's friend from Texas," said Tony.

"To the Trachepaines of New Orleans, thank you for Marie." Zack responded.

Tony and Julia appeared self-conscious.

Heads tilted slightly to consume the wine.

Zach's training prohibited the consumption of alcoholic beverages. But he thought, what the hell, a glass of wine here and bottle of beer there wouldn't do him in. So, why did he feel guilty? He realized that the Tranchepaines were graciously entertaining him and had served a sumptuous meal, treating him like a family member of the *crème de le crème* of New Orleans high society.

This dinner unfolded quite differently from his home Sunday dinners of roast beef, mashed potatoes, black eyed peas, corn-on-the-cob, pickled beets, corn bread and iced tea. The fare usually got topped off with a piece of apple pie and coffee. Not too shabby.

A gourmand at heart, Zach thoroughly enjoyed the main course. Dessert of *crème brulee* and cinnamon bread pudding topped everything off perfectly.

"Would you like coffee, *Monsieur?*" asked Liz.

"Yes, I like coffee, especially *café au lait*." He smiled at Marie.

With dessert and coffee consumed, the Tranchepaines and Zach left the table. Both Marie and her mother excused themselves.

"Would you care for a game of snooker or eight ball? I have tables for either one," Tony challenged Zach.

Tony thought to himself, you can tell a lot about a man around a snooker table.

"Whatever you prefer, I like them both," responded Zach.

"Here, have a Havana."

"Thanks."

Zach and the Baron fired up.

They walked into the Baron's game room. Zach spied the gun case. Two facing red leather chairs held court in the corner of the room. Books were neatly arranged in floor to ceiling bookshelves. A ladder on runners stood in the corner available to retrieve books from the top shelves. A globe on a footed stand crouched nearby. A large, darkly rich mahogany desk burnished with the patina of time, faced outward.

"Let's try the snooker," said the Baron chalking up his cue stick.

Zach had taken a cue from the rack. It felt good to the touch. They both rolled snooker balls down the table to see who could get closest to the end of the table without hitting it. Tony won. Zach had to break. The red balls were already racked. Zach chalked his cue slowly, crouched and took aim slightly to the right of the top facing ball of the triangular stack. He had learned over the years that a solid hit, slightly offcenter would put the rear outside ball in a side pocket.

Zach had spent more time in the pool hall adjacent to the campus than he had in the library. Not anything to brag about. Just a matter of fact. He grasped the thick part of the cue stick and proceeded to rock the lower part of the stick gently between thumb, a curled index finger and middle finger, which along with his index and little finger he placed solidly on the table.

Wham! The balls scattered willy nilly, except the rear ball, which neatly plunged into the side pocket. Zach surveyed the table. He had a couple of cripples that he dumped in unceremoniously and managed to leave himself free for a long shot down the side of the table. He steadied himself and, with a good firm stroke, sent the ball streaming into the rear side pocket. When he looked up, he saw Marie leaning on the doorsill watching from a distance.

"Nice table you have here, Mr. Tranchepaine. The side cushions are very springy. Just like I like them," said Zach as he walked around the table, which was illuminated with a low-slung green encased billiard lamp.

Zach had dropped six balls, and Tony had yet to take his turn. On a couple of occasions, Zach had "run" a snooker table. However, his seventh shot was errant, and the Baron took over.

The Baron's first shot placed a ball neatly in a side pocket. Two more successful shots followed. A couple of competitive "sharks" went after it.

Next up, Zach placed two more balls in a pocket, and left the Baron "snookered." Anyway he looked at it, he didn't have a shot; so he laid up. Next up, Zach ran the table. Score Zach 1, Tony 0.

Tony thought to himself: the kid is good, really good.

"How about another game?"

"Rack 'em."

Tony won the next game. By that time, Marie had settled into one of the leather chairs. "He's all yours, Honey. Julia and I have to pack. Remember, we have a flight out to New York tonight. Zach, if you can play basketball as well as you can snooker, the Wave will win a few more games this year. Nice meeting you, young buddy." As he left the room, he leaned over to Marie. "See if you can beat him."

"I believe I will take him on. Rack 'em, Zach."

Zach racked the eight ball table, and gave the honor of

breaking to Marie. Zach could tell Marie played frequently because of the way she gripped the billiard cue. None of this resting the cue on the back of the hand. She blasted the balls in every direction, with two of them falling in pockets.

They had scarcely begun when Zach heard a car engine outside the house. Apparently, Marie's parents were leaving for the airport.

Marie moved around the table and took a position that further revealed her figure in the black dress; thus distracting his attention away from the game at hand. She expertly dropped three balls before missing, but she left Zach a poor position from which to shoot. Turn about, fair play. He left Marie an equally poor position.

"Ball in the side pocket," as she banked one home. And finally, "eight ball in corner pocket."

Thunk, in it went.

"The loser gets to kiss the winner, rules of the game," proclaimed Zach.

Marie was receptive, and they embraced. She liked Zach's soft lips, his sweet-tasting breath and masculinity.

Earlier in the afternoon Zach had removed his coat and tie and rolled his white shirtsleeves up to just below the elbow, revealing tapered wrists and muscled forearms.

"Zach, if you will excuse me, I am going to change out of this dress. Make yourself at home. You might find a book you like in Daddy's library."

He found the big red leather chair quite comfortable. Glancing upward, he spotted burled walnut dueling pistols—relics from a different age. A couple of books lay on the reading tables.

One was by Vicomte Francois Auguste René de Chateaubriand. He thought that was a steak, not an author. He picked up another book entitled *Emile* by Jacque Rousseau. Prof Duflot had mentioned Rousseau. Something about the savage native and living naturally. He also remembered Rousseau writing about Paris and other big cities, how they had grown corrupt from various influences.

Music began to filter through the house. He recognized "Somebody Loves Me; I Wonder Who; Maybe It's You."

Marie rejoined Zach. "Come Zach, a musical interlude awaits you." Marie had changed into a white silk robe, and gently led Zach into her *boudoir*, which consisted of a sitting room, bathroom and bedroom. Zach seated himself in the sitting room, which was decorated in soothing shades of cream with furnishings of stone and iron. Antiques added interest to this expansive, now moon dappled, room. Zach sat in a Charles I side chair constructed of oak and leather.

Marie changed the records on the Victrola. On the changer she placed Glenn Miller's "String of Pearls,"Artie Shaw's "Begin the Beguine," Harry James "One O'Clock Jump," and Eddie Condon's "O Lady be Good," Zach glanced at the Condon album. Eddie Condon, guitar; Max Kaminsky, trumpet; George Wettling, drums; Jack Teagarden, trombone; Pee Wee Russell, clarinet; Ernie Caceras, sax; Bob Haggart, bass; and Jess Stacy, piano. This album was quite a revelation to Zach who, back in Dallas during his adolescent days, had brought in Eddie Condon's Saturday afternoon jazz concerts from New York on his faithful old Philco radio. Zach noticed another album by George Wettling's Chicago Rhythm Kings. This was too good to be true. Marie, a soul mate in Dixieland Jazz.

Zach, relaxed and feeling good, took Marie's hand, and they

glided into an impromptu Jitterbug to "String of Pearls." "Dah-da-da-, da-dada-da." Marie hummed as she took a backward step, and she and Zach semi-curtsied to one another. Marie had to stop dancing a time or two to tie the sash around her loose fitting gown more tightly.

The two, becoming one, glided along to "Begin the Beguine," their bodies etched in closeness. Again, the hint of Marie's perfume enchanted Zach.

They sat out "One O'Clock Jump" with an iced tea.

Marie moved toward the record player. "These are my favorite twin songs; the first for you because your eyes are telling me you want to linger." The slow blues drag, "I Want To Linger" began playing on the Victrola. The record was by Pete Daily's Dixieland Band. Pete's punching cornet led. The brassy slide of the tailgate tromboner followed along, with the solo clarinet riding high. Marie swayed across the room. Zach caught her hand, pulled her toward him, and seated her on his lap. Her rosy lips called enticingly to him. At first a light taste, then a lingering one that finished with the record.

Marie arose from Zach's lap. "And now the next song is from me to you. Why don't you 'Just Linger Awhile.'"

George Lewis' clarinet took the lead, followed by Kid Howard on trumpet and Jim Robinson on trombone. This up tempo two-stepping number caused Marie to entertain Zach with a Charleston. All she needed was a flapper dress and headband.

Incredible! What style and grace, thought Zach, who reached for another kiss.

"Not here, Zach." Marie led Zach through the bedroom and into a handsome bathroom. The floors were dark stained marble.

The oversized round basin tub was framed by graceful twisting columns. Candles with subdued lighting and soft music permeated the setting.

Marie left Zach to draw water. With graceful aplomb, she poured a fragrant lavender lotion into the tub. With her back to Zach, Marie unceremoniously dropped her robe and entered the bubbly tub. "Come on Zach. Will you join me?" asked Marie with innocent flair.

Zach's head began to spin. He hesitated. What was wrong with him?

This was certainly a hell of a lot better than the seat of his old blue pickup. What was he waiting for? He turned his back and, with a sense of modesty he detested, undressed. He folded his pants neatly over the oak chair. He obviously couldn't walk backward through the room and into the tub. For a brief moment, his doubting mind thrust forward the idea that maybe Marie just wanted him in the tub so they could clean up together.

He quickly cast the thought aside, along with his inhibitions.

"Well here I come, ready or not."

He eagerly settled in behind her in the expansive tub covered with sudsy foam and floating magnolia blossoms.

"Would you rub my shoulders, Zach?" asked Marie in a soft voice.

Zach began a slow massage of Marie's shoulders.

"A little lower down between the shoulder blades. Ah, yes, that's it.That feels so good," cooed Marie.

Glad to oblige, Zach gently stroked Marie's shoulders and lightly flicked her breasts with petaled blossoms that floated loose in the bubbly suds. He reached for another blossom and playfully moved it back and forth against Marie's legs. She appeared to almost float on amorous warmth and sheer joy. Zach felt lightheaded to say the least.

He brushed Marie's dark hair to one side and lightly kissed her neck. Marie spread out more fully before his eager gaze. How long had he dreamed of seeing her this way, he wondered. She leaned back against him and turned her head for a long kiss. Zach attempted to be nonchalant, but nothing in his life had prepared him for this moment in a big tub with someone like Marie.

Marie raised herself from the tub, stepped out, and picked up a towel, draping it over the side of the tub for him. Zach joined her as they dried, and hand-in-hand entered Marie's bedroom.

Marie's bed, with matching canopy and block-printed chintz bed hangings, stood in the corner of the room. A water vase and matching glasses rested on a wooden side table. A three-tiered mahogany box step sat at the side of the bed. A massive armoire nearly covered the wall on the other side of the bed.

Marie dimmed the lamp in a Napoleon Brandy box, and Zach carried her to the bed. He didn't need the box steps. Their lips met with passionate fury. Marie's breath tasted sweet with arousal. Her velvet tongue reached moist receptive depths.

Zach's rhythmic movements caused torrents of pleasure to roll over them both.

"I love you," whispered Zach.

"Love you. Whoa there, cowboy. We have all night."

Dawn came with the clanging of a distant streetcar on St. Charles Avenue. When Zach awoke, he found Marie staring at the ceiling. What was she thinking? He wondered.

His strength, deftness and potent thrust had pleased her, thought Marie. His tenderness afterward left her with an extraordinary sense of well being and fulfillment. She turned and leaned toward Zach when she felt him move, and they met each other in an embrace.

After a quick morning bath, they seated themselves for breakfast.

"Good morning, Miss Marie and Mr. Zach," said a cheery Liz. She placed ham, scrambled eggs, biscuits, éclairs and tarts before them. "How about some coffee?"

"Yes, thank you." Zach quaffed the brew and looked over at Marie. She had dressed in skirt, blouse, white anklet socks and penny loafers. She had a fresh scrubbed and bright-eyed look about her that he loved.

"Did Mother and Daddy say when they would return from New York?" She posed the question to Martin who had come in from the kitchen.

"Tuesday or Wednesday, I believe."

"I have classes most of the day, but should be home around four."

"I have a nine o'clock class this morning. What time is it?" inquired Zach.

"Eight o'clock, Mr. Zach."

Marie decided to walk with Zach to Tulane, before she went on to Loyola. They walked along St. Charles Avenue making small talk and plans for the next weekend. Zach's basketball games occurred mostly on Wednesday and Friday nights. If he didn't have an away game, he was usually free on Saturdays and Sundays. Sometimes he had shoot-around on Sunday afternoon.

The moss clinging to the old cypress trees on St. Charles Avenue had always intrigued Zach. Already a sixth sense told him it would be better to care for Marie rather than cling to her. He would give her room, but not too much. Their relationship felt more intimate to Zach as he walked along the avenue. Emotional tensions had lessened, and their body language was relaxed. His feelings for Marie had deepened; he sensed that she felt the same way.

Marie had delivered Zach from advanced boyhood to manhood. Up to this point Zach's life had been pretty misguided in the faux nobility of absolute inhibitionary control of his urges. He thought to himself of a past littered with wasted opportunities. Damn!

It's human nature to think wisely and act foolishly.
--Anatole France, novelist

Chapter 12
▼▼▼

"We have Georgia Tech at our place Wednesday night," Zach told Marie as they reached the Tulane campus. "It's a big game for us. If you will come, I'll leave a ticket for you again at the same place."

Marie did not hesitate, "I liked the last game a lot. I'll be there. You can count on it."

They exchanged a light kiss. Marie moved on to Loyola, and Zach sprinted for his dorm, changed into his jeans and denim shirt and slid into his seat on the first row of Prof Duflot's sociology class at 9 o'clock sharp.

Pinky Jackson leaned over. "Where've you been? Thought about sending a search party out for you."

"Tell you later," said Zach with a big smile.

Prof Duflot liked to loosen the class up with a little small talk while sitting on the side of a lecture table. He never used the lectern that sat on it. He was informal but to the point. "We are going to talk about cultural differences today. A culture is comprised of peoples mores, habits, thoughts, arts, beliefs and institutions. Sometimes we add ethnologic, ethnographic and linguistic data for a complete and comprehensive look at culture."

Pinky raised his hand. "What was that first ethno?"

"Ethnographic, meaning a socio-economic system," replied the professor. "Cultures possess similar and dissimilar characteristics. Life can be interpreted in many ways, and it manifests itself as a culture. In Hegel's *Dialectic* we learn that for every thesis there is an anti-thesis, and out of this comes a new synthesis. Synthesis in political, social, economic and metaphysical life leads to change; this is why cultures vary. The synthesis is not always the same.

Darwin points out in his *Origin of the Species* that survival comes from what works best and is strongest. This is through physical survival as well as biological survival.

A pragmatist builds upon the view that life is relative and cultures then emerge in relationship to adaptations that appear beneficial and work. Man then creates and discards ideas about who he is and how he should be and live.

The classical idealist (ideaists) would say that culture is derived from eternal truths and verities not subject to change or adaptation. The thinking here is that truth about how to live and what to do is revealed or given and is not subject to whimsical or capricious thinking. You don't create truth about bestness, you discover or encounter it in its predetermined state. A culture that is practicing "truthful" ways and means would live according to permanent and immutable laws or axioms. Now the classical realist would take this a little bit further saying that a culture would live "truthfully" if what is known in the culture is tangible. That is, empirically it can be seen, touched, observed or manipulated.

Back to the pragmatist who would only say that it all depends on existing factors; is it useful, and are needs satisfied. All cultures exist with the dilemma of knowing what is available to know (the ontological question). How is it known (the epistemological question). People in tribes, communities, states and nations work through these questions in some manner and form, and the result is what we call culture."

Zach furiously took notes from this Ph.D sociology/philosophy professor from the University of Chicago. The lecture thoroughly engrossed him, although he did not understand all of these new words and concepts. However, he did know enough to ask, and Prof Duflot patiently explained. Zach enjoyed "thinking" about things, especially abstractions. Prof Duflot's lectures helped move Zach along the pathway from mere student to scholar. His intellectual horizons expanded daily at Tulane.

Zach kept good notes, which he studied along with his textbook. Mid-term finals were coming up. He was a solid "B" student, but could become an "A" student with additional study and application. Zach could hold his own in the classroom as well as the basketball court.

Zach moved on to his English literature class. Currently, he was studying Sir Thomas Moore's *Utopia*. He had written an essay on the book, and professor Madyline Smith returned it to him in class.

She had scrawled a big red A- on the front paper. Dr. Smith rarely, if ever, gave A's, so Zach felt pretty good. On the inside of his cover page he found a note. "You write in a vigorous, vivid, graceful style, tinged with humor showing keen observation and pleasure in a well turned phrase. However, you tend to ramble somewhat. Also, learn to discipline your imagination with a few more facts."

Zach wondered if that constituted a nice way of saying that he didn't know what he was writing about. But the very last sentence stunned him: "Have you ever thought about writing as a career?"

Zach was dimly aware that Dr. Smith was a novelist as well as professor of English. Her comments made him aware that he had an opportunity to catch hold of the literary world, if only his present intellectual needs would move him in that direction. However, at his age, blocking out the roar of popular culture in order to ascend into heightened awareness of literary thought seemed an impossible task.

Later on in the afternoon Zach joined his teammates for basketball workout. He and a couple of other players horsed around imitating the Harlem Globetrotters. Zach portrayed Marques Haynes and Glenn Braden Goose Tatum. It was a riot until Coach Wells walked onto the floor. Burlesqued movements and behind the back passes were not fundamentally sound, but they sure were fun. Zach was a complex person with a humorous as well as a serious side.

After the coach arrived, the team worked on the full court press. They would attempt to disrupt Georgia Tech's patented fast break. The practice grew long and arduous. Zach was in good shape, and he could take whatever Coach could dish out.

"We will have a light workout tomorrow; go over our defensive assignments and have a shoot-around," Coach Wells instructed.

Back in the dormitory, Pinky pursued Zach's whereabouts the past weekend. "You must have the bad sweet a___. Tell your ole roomy about her."

"You met her after the LSU game."

"Her?"

"Yes, her!"

"Nice."

Zach hit the books hard but found himself feeling more interested in seeing Marie than playing basketball. And nothing had ever been more important than basketball. He had it all now, Dixieland Jazz, basketball, studies and "his woman." Or was she? Something seemed mysterious about Marie. He couldn't quite put his finger on it.

Game time rolled around. The crowds packed into the Tulane Gym. The players of the Ramblin' Wreck from Georgia Tech warmed up on one end and the Green Wave on the other.

The opening jump ball went to Georgia Tech. They started their offense with the guard around play. Zach anticipated it and switched off of his man and drew a charging foul. He made the free throw good. Georgia Tech and Tulane exchanged baskets and tied 15-15 by the end of the first quarter. At the time out, Zach looked for Marie. He spotted her in the stands and nodded. How could you miss her? Zach played his usual good floor game and had 10 points at halftime.

"They are killing us on the boards. Block out. Stay with your man until you go up for the ball," said Coach Wells.

The team rested and returned to the floor for the second half. The Tulane Pep Band brought them back with a rousing welcome. Zach opened the second half with a couple of 10-foot jumpers and put Tulane into the lead. The game wore on with neither side able to establish a significant lead. Five minutes to go, and the score was Tulane 38, Georgia Tech 39. One minute to go – tied at 45-45.

Coach Wells called time out.

"Hold the ball with our delay game. Open up the middle. Boudreau, I want you to drive the middle lane. If they don't pick you up, go all the way for a lay up. They may foul you. Otherwise, pass off to an open man. Jackson or LaSalle, take the jumper, and then follow if it's missed. Okay. Let's go."

Tulane delayed until they only had 10 seconds left, and Boudreau drove the lane. Zach threw Boudreau's blocked lay up back up onto the basket. The buzzer sounded. Game's over. Tulane 47 – Georgia Tech 45. Pandemonium reigned.

Zach took off his soaked uniform and showered. After showering and dressing, perspiration continued to stream from his face.

"Nice game, Zach. Way to go," praised Coach Wells.

"Thanks, Coach," Zach said as he wiped his face dry.

Marie waited for Zach on the gym floor. He pushed through well-wishers to join her courtside.

"Great game, Zach. You look beat."

"Not so beat that I can't take you to the after game Wave dance. What do you think?"

"Let's do it," and they were off. The dance was in the ballroom of Randall Hall.

On the way to Randall Hall, Zach slowed Marie's pace and turned her toward him. She lifted her head and met his lips with hers. Bells and whistles went off in Zach's head. He wondered about Marie.

"Love ya, Zach," she said.

They moved on to Randall Hall, a girls' dorm. The crowd had already started to gather. No live band tonight, but the record player and accompanying speakers were in place.

Zach had been dating Leslie Ann Howard. Her eye caught Zach's as he walked in with Marie on his arm, obviously curious. Zach hadn't called Leslie Ann since Christmas Break. She had a date with George Woosley on this particular evening. Zach looked quickly in her direction and then away.

Tommy Dorsey's "Opus No. 1" blared from the speakers. The Lindy Hop seemed the dance of choice. Marie and Zach went quickly into this Jitterbugging fad. They danced in smooth coordination. They dug each other's jive. Marie had a rhythm and style all her own, and Zach loved it. "In the Mood", a number by Glenn Miller, followed "Opus". Zach and Marie proved they could handle this too. Marie's little jump back curtsey jive got Zach. They visited the punch bowl table. He could get harder stuff outside the dorm, but didn't. They seated themselves in two of the chairs that ringed the dance floor.

"You're a great dancer, Zach."

"So are you, Marie. Nobody better."

Time slipped by. The next to last number for the evening was "I'll Be Seeing You," and Zach and Marie held each other tight, with Zach stealing an occasional nibble of the ear. And finally, the last number of the evening came.

Good night sweet heart,
till we meet again,
. . . . . .
Good night sweet heart,
good night.

Pinky came by with his date, Rosy Linehart. They both had red hair and made a perfect match.

"Marie you have already met Pinky, this is Rosy Linehart, and Rosy this is Marie Tranchepaine." Rosy and Marie exchanged pleasantries, and Zach pulled Pinky off to the side.

"Could you and Rosy give Marie and me a lift to her house tonight? I'm bushed."

"Sure thing." replied Pinky.

Pinky had acquired a '40 model Chevy four-door from his father, which had become a favorite mode of transportation for most of the Tulane basketball team.

"I'll get our coats and meet you in the parking lot," explained Zach.

"Okay."

Marie and Rosy tidied up in the women's room and joined Zach and Pinky outside. Rosy hailed from Shreveport and, like Pinky, had entered her sophomore year at Tulane.

Soon, Pinky had the Chevy pointed down St. Charles Avenue. Marie and Zach nestled together in the back seat. Zach ached with tiredness, but he enjoyed Marie's company.

"Go on up to the next street and turn around, my house is the second on the right," directed Marie.

Pinky followed directions and came to a stop at the appropriate house, His eyes widened, and he arched his brow at Zach as Zach left the car with Marie.

"Remember, Saturday night at the Famous Door."

Marie agreed with a nod, and reached up around Zach's neck for a goodnight kiss. "Goodnight sweetheart, good night."

Chapter 13
▼▼▼

Saturday evening rolled around. Zach borrowed Pinky's car and picked Marie up at 7 p.m. They stopped at the Pearl Café on St. Charles Avenue for a PoBoy sandwich made with oysters, mayonnaise, sauce piquant, tomatoes and onions.

"Go light on the onions," cautioned Zach to the waiter. A bottle of Jax beer tasted just right for the duo.

Marie was her usual fresh scrubbed charming self. She had pulled back her hair on this evening revealing the full exquisiteness of her face.

"Did your mother and father get back from New York?" inquired Zach innocently enough, hoping that they hadn't.

"Got back Thursday," returned Marie.

"They are nice. Be sure and thank them again for their hospitality last Sunday. You were pretty hospitable yourself." Zach gazed into Marie's eyes, and they finished their PoBoy's in this manner.

"It was my pleasure, to be sure," cooed Marie in a slow sultry manner.

The opening set for the evening had already begun when Marie and Zach arrived at the Famous Door on Bourbon Street.

Bunk Johnson's New Orleans Band pumped to "Darktown Strutters' Ball". Bunk led with his trumpet. Jim Robinson, with his cheeks blown out like balloons, counter attacked Bunk's every move. George Lewis played clarinet. Warren "Baby" Dodds steadied the band with his faithful drum beat; and Lawrence Marrero plunked away at his banjo. The 66-year-old grayheaded Bunk Johnson left his seated position in the middle of the band and stepped forward.

> *I'll be down to get you in a taxi, Honey.*
> *Now, Honey, don't be late.*
> *I want to be there when the band starts playin'...*

This could have been Zach's theme song, as he always wanted to be there when the band started playing.

The tempo was upbeat as Bunk returned to his seat and led the band in ensemble to a hard driving finish. Jim Robinson's trombone wailed and moaned in the background. It was hypnotic.

Marie and Zach had ringside seats at a small round table. They ordered 7-ups, which they nursed relentlessly throughout the evening.

"Here's a little ditty called 'High Society', featuring George Lewis on the clarinet," said a gravely-voiced Bunk Johnson.

Off the band went with this lively march syncopated tune. George Lewis went into his low *obligato* solo with Lawrence Marrero's banjo punctuating his song.

Marie smiled and gently swayed with the band. Zach wondered if she could possibly love this music as much as he did.

The band moved into a 1920's pop tune – "One Sweet Letter From You." Marie and Zach had to restrain themselves to keep from getting up to dance. Bunk's band finished the first set with "Franklin

Street Blues." Bunk carefully placed his horn on his chair and stepped down from the small raised stage. He lit a cigarette.

"Hello Miss Marie, and I don't believe I have the name of this young feller."

Zach held out his hand as he and Bunk shook. "Zach LaSalle."

"I've seen you in here before. You like my music?"

"Nobody plays it better. I love your trumpet."

"I got what it takes to stomp 'em. I know it yet. I'm gettin' to be an old man, but not in action and playin'."

Zach took a deep breath because he was about to take a risk on unsafe ground. But not to risk is not to live. "Mr. Johnson, I'm going to ask you something that I have wanted to do ever since I heard your band. I brought my mouthpiece with me tonight, and my trumpet is in the car. Could I try a number with your band?" Zach held his breath as it made him very nervous approaching Bunk Johnson, the king of New Orleans trumpet players.

Bunk squinted at young LaSalle and broke into a big grin. "You think you're up to it. Go get your horn."

Marie looked quite surprised. She had heard Zach talk about his band back in Dallas, but had never heard him play his horn.

"Be back in a minute."

Bunk remained at the table with Marie. "How is Kate these days? I haven't seen her lately."

"She is doing fine, Mr. Johnson. She often talks of you and the days you played for her over on Franklin Street."

"Kate was the best ever. When you see her, tell her hello and come do a number or two with us."

Zach returned with his trumpet; took it out of its case and

began to blow a little air through it as he warmed up his mouthpiece. He was jittery, but wanted desperately to try his luck with this real stuff band.

Members of the band returned from the break and once again seated themselves. Bunk invited Zach up on the stage and hurriedly noted to the band members that Zach was "sitting in" on the next number. He turned to Zach. "What do you want to play?"

"Panama".

"Good enough. In what key?"

"B flat or F."

"Let's go with B flat."

Zach hadn't played this number in some time, but it was one of his favorites. He looked around, and the musicians eyed him with some skepticism, waiting for him to give the downbeat. His throat went dry, but he launched into the first note anyway. He began with a slight falter missing a couple of notes, but found himself feeling more confident as he went along on this upbeat two-stepping rag. The feeling was glorious playing with these seasoned *crème de la crème* New Orleans jazz musicians. The music swirled around him, and he lost himself in the intricate pattern of "Panama." He drove it on home, leading the pack in the final crescendo.

Marie sat captivated. Zach was no Bunk Johnson, but he had played strongly, if not superbly. The band members gave Zach a nod of approval.

Bunk, who had been standing off to one side, approached Zach. "It don't matter if the cat is black or white, as long as it catches the mouse," and patted Zach on the shoulder.

Zach didn't want to press his luck. However, he couldn't resist asking, "Can I do one more number?"

"One more it will be."

"Let's try 'It Had To Be You.'" A more relaxed Zach put his horn to his lips and took off. The supporting rhythm gave him a feeling of confidence. He played the first four bars and then, surprising everyone including Marie, dropped his horn and looking at her, began to sing.

> *It had to be you,*
> *It had to be you.*
> *I wandered around,*
> *And finally found,*
> *Somebody who.*
> *Would make it be true,*
> *And made it be blue.*
> *And even be glad,*
> *And make me be sad,*
> *Just thinking of you.*
> *Some others I've seen,*
> *Might never be mean,*
> *. . . .*
> *For nobody else gave me a thrill,*
> *For you have no faults,*
> *Because I love you still.*
> *It had to be you,*
> *Wonderful you,*
> *It had to be you.*

Each member of the band took a solo, and Zach moved from one foot to the other keeping in beat with the band, and looking longingly at Marie.

She returned the gaze, and Zach led the band in conclusion of the number.

Zach even received scattered polite applause from those in

attendance. He thanked Bunk and his sidekicks and stepped down to rejoin Marie.

"Okay, Zach. You started it, but I'm gonna finish it."

Marie walked up the small steps on the side of the stage and approached Bunk.

"What'll it be?"

"'Don't Sweetheart Me.'"

Bunk blasted into this old time cakewalker, and Marie took center stage, and pointing her finger at Zach began:

> *Don't sweetheart me,*
> *If you don't mean it.*
> *Don't say sweet words,*
> *That are not true.*
> *Don't tear my heart,*
> *Like it was paper.*
> *Because this heart loves only you.*
> *You can't go round*
> *Sweetheartin' others,*
> *And pretend that I am your exclusively.*
> *Love must be true,*
> *Mean what you're saying.*
> *Unless you do,*
> *Don't sweetheart me.*
> *If you go struttin' around,*
> *Doin' the town,*
> *You can't go 'round*
> *Sweetheartin' others.*

Bunk and Jim Robinson went into a frenzied pulsating finish with Marie cakewalkin' and struttin' her stuff. What a performance.

Bunk stepped forward and presented Marie. "Miss Marie, isn't she wonderful. This band's not bad either. We may be old in years, but we can still play. That's stompin' 'em," said a grinning Bunk to the audience. Zach gave a salute to Marie and helped her down the side steps to tumultuous applause from the crowd at the Famous Door.

Once seated, Zach leaned forward and took Marie's hands.

"What a combination – a hoofer and a singer. You are fantastic, Marie."

"If you want more, come see me over on Chartres Street. Next week I will do a couple of numbers in the 'Red-hot Babes in Review.' It's an old time Vaudeville house with a little bit of burlesque thrown in to spice it up a bit."

"No kidding!" declared Zach in amazement. "Do they need an MC? I could get my straw hat and striped pants and be ready to go."

"What do you know about straw hats and baggy pants?" queried Marie.

The Bunk Johnson Band finished the second set with "When the Saints Go Marchin' In."

In the springtime we have a stage show out at school. I MC that show, tell some bad jokes and play in the stage band. When we make our basketball trips to Kansas City, St. Louis and Chicago, I find what's left of the Vaudeville and burlesque houses and take good notes on the comedy sketches and jokes. Clean it up a little bit and it plays quite well at school."

" What a hoot. Maybe we ought to go into show business. Come see me. I'll be appearing on Tuesday and Thursday nights."

Zach thought. A Renaissance woman – beautiful, literate, sophisticated, musically talented, sweet lovin' and fun lovin'. What a combination! Could this be happening to him? It seemed like just yesterday when Marie had pulled herself into a tight ball and slept across from him on the train ride back to New Orleans.

Zach and Marie thanked Bunk Johnson again for allowing them to perform with his band. Bunk smiled and said, "Come again. We play all the time."

Marie and Zach returned to Zach's borrowed car on the cool and damp New Orleans night. Fog had settled in, and it was difficult to see, driving Marie back to her home. They crept along and Elegante de Arms soon came into view. The black Chevy sputtered to a stop. Zach turned off the ignition and doused the lights before he turned to accept a sweetened liquid kiss from Marie. Lingering kisses steamed up their cocooned car, forming a light dew inside the windows.

"I better go in, Love," whispered Marie. "I had a wonderful time."

"When can I see you again?" asked Zach.

"Call me," responded Marie.

Zach walked Marie to her door and embraced her with a long goodnight kiss.

"Love ya."

"Love, ya, too."

Zach started up his old pal's car. He was giddy with affection for Marie and wondered if she felt the same.

Chapter 14
▼▼▼

    This Sunday passed in a much calmer fashion for Zach than his last. He studied, and horsed around with his basketball teammates. The week before him was pretty much in place. Classes, another home game with Georgia on Wednesday and a trip to Shreveport with a non-conference game with Centenary on Friday.
    Relentlessly, he called for Marie the first part of the week. No luck. He remembered that Marie would perform at the Red-hot Babes Review on Tuesday. He planned to catch her act. Tuesday evening rolled around, and he caught the streetcar down to Canal Street and looked for the "Palace" showplace on Chartres. Flashing neon lights helped him find it. He handed over a 50-cent piece and entered the dimly lit Palace Theatre.
    Indented lights along the seats helped him find his way down the middle aisle. High-backed wooden seats lined up in rows flanked the middle and only aisle, which contained a small runway that extended halfway out and above the seats. People from all walks of life filled the theatre to near capacity. Zach spotted his science professor seated down a few rows and in front of him.

The stage lights came on, the curtain went up and the Ragtime Pit Band blasted forth with "Brass Bells," ushering in seven Red-hot Babes including Marie, who centered in front of the group. They danced steadily to a shag cakewalk. What atmosphere. Marie, in tight halter and dancing shorts, led the pack in this gusto number. After the number concluded with a rush, Zach sank back in his seat with locked eyeballs. Whew.

The master of ceremonies came on stage and fanned the girls with his straw hat as they made their retreat. After the last one exited, he turned and did an easy pratfall over a piece of luggage. "Just getting over the grip," he said. Rim shot. "Good evening ladies and gentlemen, welcome to the Palace Theatre where the girls are gorgeous and ...,"

"Well bring 'em back," hollered a heckler.

"Did you pay to get in, Sir?"

"No, but I'll pay to get out, if you don't bring back the girls." Rim shot.

Muffled laughter rippled through the crowd.

"Introducing the Step Brothers. Here they are in person," announced the MC.

The pit band roared with "Everybody Loves My Baby," and the four dancers in black suits and top hats hit the stage with their taps echoing a staccato cadence. One by one attempted to outdo one another with improvisations. They finished with a flourish and a big round of applause. The curtain fell and then reopened to a court scene. The judge pounded his gavel, but nobody paid attention, until the accused came in amidst tassels, bells and whistles.

The puffed up prosecutor intoned, "Your honor, this hussy, Lulu Belle Jones, is accused of indecent exposure." Rim shot.

"I don't give a diddly squat what she is accused of, she is not guilty," said her grave defender.

"Diddly, who did what?" questioned the judge with mock seriousness.

"Your Honor, he squatted."

"Squatted where?"

"I rise to a point of law."

"You're lucky to rise from that chair."

In the meantime Lulu Belle joined the jury, which paid more attention to her than they did the judge.

The curtain came down, and the MC announced, "Ladies and gentlemen, another example of jurisprudence in our fair city. And now I call your attention to the lovely, the incomparable, the most gorgeous of all – Madam Tonya."

The stage lights dropped, and a spotlight hit the center of the curtain, which slowly rose. With a long razzing slide from the trombone, the band blazed forth with the slow drag, "Riverside Blues." Madam Tonya, dressed in a flowing purple gown with feathers all about moved slowly, but sensuously forward. She glided to one side, paused and posed, then removed a white glove and tossed it aside. Then she made a few slow struts to the other side of the stage. The other glove came off. In the center of the stage she slowly shimmied and removed her gown. Now down to a G-string and tassels, she strutted up the runway to the ever pounding beat of the pit band. A bump here – rim shot; and a bump there – rim shot. Shakin' and shimmy'n, she went back to center stage. Madam Tonya pranced wildly back and forth as the slow drag blues came to a halt. She removed a pastie, but the MC covered up with a fallen feather. She clicked her leg back with a saucy exit and disappeared into the recesses of the stage. Curtain down, the crowd roared.

"Yes, she is tantalizing, Madam Tonya."

The curtain came up, and Madam Tonya came back amidst feathers, blowing the audience a kiss. The band struck up, and she reluctantly left the stage.

The MC positioned himself, authoritatively, "Tonight, ladies and gentlemen, we have a special treat for you. Introducing for the first time at the Palace our very own sizzling and syncopating Marie Tranchepaine singing the 'Blues My Naughty Sweetie Gives to Me.'"

The band struck up, and Marie entered from the side in a tight fitting outfit leaving little to the imagination. Zach recognized the scintillating body. She danced and cakewalked with cane and hat in hand, and sang with a strong voice.

> *There are blues that you get from worry.*
> *There are blues that you get from pain.*
> *There are blues when you're lonely,*
> *For your one and only,*
> *The blues you can never explain.*
> *There are blues that you get from longing.*
> *But the bluest blues that be,*
> *Are thought of as blues of mine,*
> *But they are the very meanest kind,*
> *The blues my naughty sweetie gave to me.*

The Red-hot Babes joined Marie, and they finished with a flourish. A long ovation ensued, led by Zach LaSalle.

Intermission.

The house lights came up, and a pitchman moved along the aisle. "Peanuts. Candy. Peanuts. Candy."

Zach stretched and looked for the bathroom. Moving through

the small lobby, Dr. Lovelady smiled as Zach glanced his way.

The 15-minute delay concluded and the house lights went dim again. The band struck up the "Maple Leaf Rag" and the Red-hot Babes hit the stage with another high-steppin' number.

"Aren't they wonderful?" intoned the MC. "And for your listening pleasure up from Tishomingo, Mississippi, Mr. Nat Jones."

Mr. Jones took the stage in tie and tails, and the band began a soft lilting introduction.

Gone to Tishomingo,
Because I'm sad today.
I wish to labor,
Way down old Dixie way.
Oh my weary heart,
Cries out in pain.
Oh how I wish that I was back again,
With those rains, in the plains,
Where they make you welcome all the time.
Way down in Mississippi,
Amongst the cypress trees.
Take what you give me,
With that strange melody.
To resist temptation,
I just can't refuse.
Way down in Tishomingo,
I wish to linger,
Where they play those weary blues.
I'm goin' to Tishomingo,
Because I'm sad today.
I wish to labor,
Way down old Dixie way.
Oh my weary heart cries out in pain,
Way down in Mississippi,

In Tishomingo,
I wish to linger,
Where they play those weary blues.

Mr. Jones finished with a soft-shoe shuffle, and the band took him home – presumably to Tishomingo.

Out came the Babes to "Smokey Hokes."

"If they were any hotter, the stage would catch on fire." The MC had a million of them.

A bad comedian followed the girls, so bad he got the hook. Zach thought, I could do better.

The MC, in his effervescence, announced, "For our final show stoppin' number, we have saved Miss Tranchepaine and the Red-hot Babes in 'I Ain't Gonna Give Nobody None of My Jelly Roll'. Jelly Roll Morton are you listenin'?"

I ain't gonna give nobody none of my jelly roll.
No I wouldn't give you a piece of this cake,
Not to save your soul.
Mama told me today before she went away,
She would bring me a toy,
Because I'm Mama's pride and joy.
Ain't no use for you to keep hanging around.
You know that love I gave you,
Gonna turn you down.
Now your jelly roll may be sweet,
But mine just can't be beat.
So I ain't gonna give you,
You can't have none,
Of my jelly roll.

The girls and the band finished rollicking and kicking and

brought the house down. The curtain came down, but went back up and the Babes stepped forward kicking and bowing. The band ushered them back, the curtain lowered again and the lights went on.

The sight mesmerized Zach, and he sat enthralled. Wow, he wanted some more of Marie's sweet jelly roll. He waited for the crowd to move slowly from the theatre. He moved down toward the stage in great anticipation of seeing Marie. Pandemonium and confusion reigned. "May I see Miss Tranchepaine?" Zach asked the stage director.

"Please wait. Have a seat, and I will tell her you're here. What is your name?"

"Zach LaSalle."

"Just a minute."

Five minutes passed, and Zach decided to move back stage. Upon entering, Zach caught a glimpse of Marie, wrapped in a fur coat, leaving on the arm of a man through a side door. Surely that wasn't Marie. Yes it was. He peered in amazement as Marie and the man entered a black Buick convertible and drove off.

Chapter 15
▼▼▼

Long sharp fingernails gently tapped Zach on the shoulder. He turned abruptly and stood face-to-face with a lady and gentleman. He thought he recognized the lady, but had never seen the man.

"Mr. Zach, that is your name, isn't it?" "Yes it is."

"Remember me, Kate Robicheaux. I'm Marie's carre Mama, and this is my husband Andre Robicheaux."

Zach shook hands with them both. "Now I remember, last week listening to Kid Ory's band."

"You got it. I wouldn't look for Marie tonight, son. You hungry? Come on, you can cry in your beer over at Andre's place. He might even serve you a gastronomic goodie or two."

Zach attempted to recover from the shock of seeing Marie leave the theatre with another man. He expressed his appreciation for the offer. "Thank you, but I probably ought to get back to school. Have a game tomorrow night."

"You ridin' the trolley or you gotta car?" quizzed Andre.

"I'll walk back to Canal and take the streetcar back out to school," asserted Zach.

"Oh come on with us Zach, Andre can take you home in a little while, can't you, Honey."

Andre shrugged in compliance.

Zach relented and eased into the back seat of Andre's white Packard convertible.

"Didja enjoy the show tonight?" asked Kate.

"Loved it, especially Marie. She is so talented."

"Takes after her Mama, boy," said a proud Kate. "Kate and Marie been dancin' these streets a long time. Right, Andre?"

"Right, Katy."

"Me and Marie talk all the time. She tells me you play a mean ole trumpet."

"I try, but I'm not up to the Quarter standards. If I were good enough, I would play down here all the time."

Andre turned on Iberville and pulled in front of "Acme" denoted by a big blueish neon sign. A smaller sign flashed "Beer and Oysters by the Bucket." Below that "Meade Lux Lewis playing Nitely."

Kate and Zach got out, and Andre disappeared into the darkness in his Packard. Zach had never been on Iberville Street. This was new territory. Kate led Zach into the Acme. The pungent odor of oysters and beer greeted him at the door.

A big man pumped away at the piano. Andre appeared from out of the kitchen. Zach could see him better now. He looked dressed out in a pinstripe suite. A long chain dangled from his pocket. His trousers were baggy but cut tight at the bottom. Kate settled Zach at a table near the piano man.

Andre came to the table. "Ah got you some beer and oysters, young buddy."

Could I have a PoBoy sandwich and tea, instead?" asked Zach.

"Tea," snorted Andre. "Beer is more better. Oh well." He motioned for a waiter. "Get this young feller a PoBoy and bring it right chere."

"Lux, would you play the 'Honky Tonk Train Blues?'" asked Kate as she lit a cigarette and blew smoke upward and way from Zach's still somewhat boyish and questioning face. Kate leaned forward. "My Marie is complicated. She is reposited in time. Tranchepaine and Iberville blood run in her veins. She has a strange exotic sense of belonging here as well as up on the avenue. You must go slow with her, my boy, or she will break your heart. Your eyes betray you when it comes to Marie."

Hearing Kate talk about Marie sent a spontaneous and uncontrollable shiver through Zach.

Lux finished his boogie woogie, Honky Tonk number, and Kate gave him a thumbs up gesture. Kate had a fluidness about her motions that reminded Zach of Marie. However, her speech came out exaggerated and animated. Earlier, Marie's body had moved ever so subtly to the tinkle of the ivory keys. She fascinated Zach.

"I came to see the show tonight, but didn't have a date with Marie."

"You don't date Marie, Zach, you experience her. She is like a hummingbird, moving from one nectar to the other. She doesn't stay in one place too long; however, she may come back.

She left this evening with Jacque Buisson, an heir to considerable property in the Garden District. It is said that long ago a Buisson was one of Napoleon's Lieutenants who surveyed and designed the village of Lafayette where Jacque now owns this property. They were engaged to be married last year. Marie broke off the engagement, but they continue to see one another.

Zach's PoBoy wasn't going down very good. "I believe I better go. How much is my sandwich?"

"On the house, if you will come back."

"Sure thing", said Zach.

"I'll get Andre to take you home." She turned and looked for Andre. "Don't see him."

"That's okay." Zach thought he should get back to the dorm and get some sleep before tomorrow night's game. Coach Wells didn't do bed checks. He trusted that his players would discipline themselves. Zach felt a little guilty.

"Bye Kate, and thanks for the sandwich talk."

Kate patted his hand and showed him to the door.

The night air felt good. It was a relief to get away from the cigarette and cigar smoke in the Acme. The street had grown damp with fog. He had not ventured this far north in the Quarter before. He hurriedly walked up Iberville to Rampart Street. He wondered if bands had swayed down this street to the Rampart Street Parade. He felt alone along the deserted street. He had learned from experience to walk close to the street and way from buildings. On one occasion, a man with stubs for arms had pinned him to a building. The man released him after he agreed to turn over his pocketbook.

Soon he found Canal. It seemed like a long way to the street station. Maybe he should have waited for Andre. Too late for that. He broke into a trot. Life had taught him a lesson today. This was an important part of his education. The only difference between this experience and Tulane was he got credit toward a degree for things that happened to him at school. Finally he settled onto the streetcar headed home. Classes and basketball were on his itinerary for the remainder of the week, but Marie danced in his head.

Chapter 16
▼▼▼

Zach made his classes, frequented the library every once in a while, shot pool with his buddies, and occasionally dated Leslie Ann Howard. However, Marie never drifted far from his thoughts. Liz usually answered his phone calls to the Tranchepaine residence. He received the stock answer. "Miss Marie is not taking calls," she would say, politely.

Zach attended several more shows at the Palace Theatre. Marie performed, scintillating as ever. He figured that if Marie didn't want to see him, he wouldn't press the issue.

The middle of February rolled around and the Tulane Green Wave fell into the home stretch for the championship of the Southeastern Conference. Only Kentucky blocked their path. The final game of the season was in Lexington. Zach and his teammates drove to Lexington in two DeSoto station wagons, which were longer than a French Quarter block. They stacked basketballs and other playing gear high on top. Basketball trips made for a long haul. Zach took along a couple of books to study. However, procrastination usually eclipsed his good intentions. It was hard to study in a hotel room when horseplay ruled the day.

Zach ate his pre-game meal at 5:30 p.m. A slice of roast beef, baked potato, green beans and pancakes for dessert. This meal would give him the energy to take on the Kentucky Wildcats. The trainer came into his room at 6 p.m. for ankle taping. He applied some awful-smelling yellow pre-adhesive solution to both ankles. He then attached anchor strips – one high on the ankle, the other just above the toes. Rip, went the tape. Trainer Metz LaFollete then moved to a figure eight steadily enclosing the ankle in a rigid cast of tape.

Jockstrap preceded Zach's playing shorts. He neatly tucked his undershirt style jersey inside his shorts. On came the green and white warm-up jacket and pants. Placing a white hotel towel neatly inside his jacket collar completed his suiting up. He felt like a warrior ready to do battle. A small bus transported the team from the hotel to the Kentucky field house already full of fans when they arrived. Coach Wells took his team into the visitors locker room for pre-game instructions.

"We have worked all week getting ready for these guys. We'll use our trapping defense to start the game, and try to slow down their fast break. If Beard gets that thing goin', we're in a heap of trouble. Let's go get warmed up."

The Wave took the floor and started with easy-going single file crip shots, which gradually gave way to random individual spot shooting. Zach felt good. His jumpers swished the nets.

Kentucky took the floor to a maddening roar. "On, Blue and White" went the band, outfitted in blue and white striped blazers. Kentucky proved themselves tough competition. They took their basketball seriously, and expected to win, and they usually did. They usually made it to the national champions.

Braden out-jumped Groza, and Tulane took the ball down quickly and, after faking a fast break, set up their single post offense that consisted of drives and cuts off Braden who handled the ball on the post. Zach had a hard time getting the ball to Braden as Groza fronted him. Zach tried a lob pass over Groza's outstretched arms. Two points. Braden put it home. In running back on defense, Zach noticed Coach Rupp off the bench, face red, giving Groza the once over. At half time – Kentucky 36, Tulane 31.

"We have a good chance. We can beat these guys, if you want it badly enough. Zach, keep taking your jumpers. Boudreau, your shots will begin to fall. Don't hesitate. We've got to have three men on the boards at all times.'

Zach did his best at rebounding, Groza loosened one of his teeth with an unfortunately placed elbow. The game proved tough going. Zach took a last drink of water from a weak fountain.

It appeared to Zach that Kentucky shot quite a number of free throws. Anytime you go on the road, you figure to get the short end of the officiating, They call it Homering. Coach Wells stood his ground with the officials. The Green Wave was simply out-manned on this cold winter night in Lexington, Kentucky. Final score, Kentucky 64, Tulane 45. However, the Green Wave finished the season with a good record of 22 wins and 9 losses.

Zach wearily returned with the team to their hotel. As he opened the hotel room door, an envelope fell to the floor. "Zach LaSalle," read the ink on the front of the envelope in very neat handwriting. He opened it and removed a card that read – "I will dance in your bed tonight. Beware, you cannot get away from me." Zach eased down on his hotel bed. Dance in my bed tonight? Strange. He tossed the card aside and slowly removed his uniform.

Metz LaFollete came into the room and cut the tape off his ankles. His heartbeat felt rapid enough from the effects of the ballgame, but it seemed to speed up a little bit more after he read the note. He stayed under the shower a long time, washing off the day and night's activities.

"Get the hell out of the shower or there won't be any hot water left," admonished Pinky, standing ready at the shower stall.

"It's all yours." Zach toweled off, went to his bed and read the note again. He ordered a sandwich from room service. He had five dollars for an after game snack.

The hotel room felt cold, but he finally got the bed warm and attempted to fall asleep. He could not. Too much adrenaline continued to flow through his veins. Beware of whom? He thought.

He eased the note under his pillow. The minutes dragged on. He glanced at the hotel clock. 2 a.m.

LaFollete woke him at 7 a.m. "Up and at 'em. Let's go. Be down for breakfast at 8 a.m. Pack your gear and bring it down so we can load up and be ready to go after breakfast."

Zach thought, if coach Wells says 8 a.m. for breakfast, that's exactly what he means.

The ride back to New Orleans tired Zach. The basketball season was over. Zach and Pinky trudged back to their dorm. He found another unopened, but this time stamped, envelope on the little table by his bed. What's going on here? Was this another dance in his bed note?

The envelope was addressed to Monsieur Zachary LaSalle.

He opened it. Neatly engraved on this silky paper he read:

> *Marie de le Tranchepaine,*
> *through the authorization*
> *of the Baron Antoinne*
> *and*
> *Baroness Julia Calve Tranchepaine,*
> *request the honor of your presence at the*
> *Mystic Krewe of Comus Ball.*
> *The soirée is to begin at 8 p.m.,*
> *Saturday, 26 February,*
> *Elegante de Arms,*
> *1938 St. Charles Avenue.*
> *Bal masque de rigueur is dress for the evening.*
>
> *RSVP.*

Zach lay down on his bed, folded his arms behind his head and stared at the ceiling...*Dance in his bed?...a soiree?* Kate had warned him. He wondered if Marie had also invited the poseur – Jack Boo – something.

Chapter 17
▼ ▼ ▼

Plans for Mardi Gras activites escalated all around. Last year Zach had casually observed the carnival parades. Now, this year Marie had invited him to the soiree at her home. Why this, he thought after all these weeks when she refused to talk to him, much less see him. He slept with visions of Marie, masks and marching street bands dancing around frantically in his head.

Pinky and Zach completed breakfast and sauntered back to their dorm room.

"Marie invited me to a soiree at her house this coming Saturday," asserted Zach.

"Not soree', but swaarae, old pal. If you can't say it, how do you think you can do it?" grinned Pinky.

"By the way, what is a bal masque de riger?" inquired Zach knowing full well Pinky didn't have a clue either.

To his astonishment, Pinky declared, "It means come dressed in a tuxedo with tails and mask. You need to work on your French."

"I never had a tux on in my life."

"You can rent 'em down the street. There is a place a couple of blocks from the campus. They got masks and everything."

The next day, Zach stepped into Pepe's Evening Wear and Costumes. The proprietor outfitted him in tux and mask. The rental cost more than he had, but he worked out a payment plan and proudly carried his masked ball uniform back to school with him that evening.

Zach entered the Liberal Arts Building and took his seat beside Leslie Ann Howard. They had signed up for the English class together.

"Hello, Zach. Sorry about the Kentucky game," Leslie Ann intoned in a consoling manner.

"Boy, it's tough over there. They wiped us out."

Dr. Madyline Smith began her lecture. "We continue today our theme of Utopia that we began with Sir Thomas Moore's work. Aristotle posed that the ultimate questions for mankind are 'who are we? What can be known? And how should we organize ourselves in living together?' Most Utopian writers deal with some aspect of these questions. Caesar Marcus Aurelius wrote that the most important thing in this life is what you choose to think about. Or, as René Descartes proclaimed, 'I think, therefore, I am.'

Great works of literature come about as people think about this life. It is a life of the mind. Take the high road in your thinking. This is difficult since our popular culture is littered with junk thought. Thomas Carlyle wrote, 'Our main business of thought is not to see what dimly lies in the distance, but apply ourselves to what clearly is at hand today.'

What you think today shapes who you are and what you will become in the future. For this reason, your list of great books to read should help fashion your own thoughts and future beliefs and actions. So select what you read and think about carefully. Be alert. Just as food nourishes the body, literature nourishes the mind."

Zach took notes, feverishly.

A hand went up. "How does one know what is 'best' to read?"

"You will need to read widely in order to enjoin the collective memory of Western Civilization. Thinkers before you have made selections that appear to stand the test of time with eternal verities and truths. And seeking truth is the noble aspiration of a writer or reader. Genuineness is prized in any work. Live your life as a painting. Your canvas is the world.

However, it is through the most commonplace objects before you that you can reach the most universal understanding. What goes on your canvas is a result of what you have read, what people have told you and what you have thought. Craft your thoughts, carefully. Writers paint a picture with words. If you love words and how they are used, then you will love writing and reading, and you will feel at home with yourself in your quest for knowledge, beauty and truth. This will center your being, for life's journey is one of curiosity, searching, discovering and creating. Whatever your purpose, reading, writing and thinking will underpin it.

Back to what books to read—listen to your inner voice, and your true character and spiritual self will emerge clarified and strong. Then follow your creative fire. Become a source of literature, rather than a derivative.

I do not know how many of you will become serious writers. However, I want you to think about it. Utopias are built through thought, writing and action. You can become part of the action of change in this world. And remember change is ambivalent and neutral. If you get involved, then you can have something to say about whether the changes are for the better or for the worse. There is no refuge from change. You will either be pragmatic and elastic, or ideological and will always seek some common ground.

Again, on the question of what best to read and think, all I can say is, live by paying attention to the human condition with empathy and how you might improve it. Think for yourself with an aspirational and inspirational voice. Do something that matters, either alone, or with others.

Cherish the day, the hour, the moment, and make the most of it. For as Carlyle wrote, 'All we have is what is in front of us.'

And last, be ferociously persistent in seeking your blisses. Here's a little story. Two frogs fell into a bucket of cream. One frog quit kicking and drowned. The other frog kicked so hard he turned the cream into butter, rose to the top and jumped out. Be persistent and work hard, and you can have your Utopia."

Zach closed his notebook. His mind felt filled to the brim with thoughts. He admired Dr. Smith. And he knew that he loved Marie.

Chapter 18
▼▼▼

Zach grew tired of riding the streetcar and borrowing Pinky's car. Pinky got tired of it, too. So, Zach arranged for an old pal needing a ride down south's way to drive and nurse his '41 model Blue Goose pickup from home down to New Orleans.

Zach picked up the phone in the lobby of the dorm when it rang.

"Is that you, Zach? This is Neal Jensen. I made it to New Orleans. How do I get to Tulane?"

"Do you know where you're calling from?"

"I'm west of the city on Highway 90."

"Good. Just keep on going east until you hit Calhoun Street, turn right and that street will bring you straight onto campus. I will walk down to the corner and flag you down. See you in a little while."

Zach waited at the corner of Claiborne and Calhoun for his pal Neal and his old Blue Goose. It wasn't long before they coasted into view. The light blue-colored pickup was unmistakable. Zach waved Neal down. Neal came to a screeching halt, and Zach jumped in on the passenger side. They shook hands, and Zach directed Neal to the dorm.

"It shore is a long way down here," asserted Neal. "Didn't think I would ever make it."

"Man, am I glad to see you."

"Glad to see me or your pickup?"

"Both."

Neal ate a sandwich with Zach in the dorm and slept the night on a makeshift pallet in Zach's room. The next day, Zach drove Neal to the train depot.

"Thanks again for bringin' ole Goose down here."

"Anytime," responded Neal with his aw shucks demeanor.

"Got to be headin' on down to 'Alibami'." Neal and Zach walked to the train platform.

"All aboard, that's goin' aboard," shouted the conductor.

Neal stepped up on the steel step and entered the train. He gave a nod to Zach and disappeared into the recesses of the cars. Zach liked Neal. They had been high school buddies in Dallas.

Zach cranked up his pickup and drove back to the campus. It was running pretty good, but needed a wash job. He would clean it up for his drive over to 1938 St. Charles Avenue.

Zach had circled Saturday, 26 February, on the calendar.

Today was the day. He messed around school, shot a game of pool with Pinky and, during the afternoon, brought in Eddie Condon's jazz concert from New York on the radio. He didn't eat much during the day because he figured the Tranchepaines might have a delicacy or two that evening.

Seven forty-five p.m. found him dressed, complete with tuxedo and tails. First time in his life.

"Hey, Pinky, when do I put this mask on?"

"Beats the hell out of me."

Zach felt slightly conspicuous when he left the dorm. He hoped none of his basketball buddies saw him. Being in the Blue Goose gave him a good feeling. He had shined it up real good, but a light rain was falling as he drove down St. Charles Avenue. There went his wash job.

As he approached Marie's house, the number of limousines lining up or pulling away from Marie's driveway took him aback. He knew of a parking space around the back of the house. He had seen Martin park there on several occasions. He pulled around behind the house, shifting jerkily from first to second. Were the gears sticking, or was he nervous? He was in luck. He found the space empty. He pulled to a stop and hoped that Martin wouldn't need the space for the evening.

Zach locked his pickup. Probably would be a lot of folks who would want to steal this prize. He walked around to the front of the house and mingled with incoming guests. To his surprise, no one wore a mask. The women were dressed in party dresses with fur coats draped about their shoulders. He hurriedly walked back to his pickup, unlocked it, and threw his mask on the seat, and returned to the front door. Julia Calve and Marie were greeting the guests as they arrived.

"Good evening, Mr. Mayor. You and Mrs. Morrison-please come in," said Julia Calve with high expectation and affection. Zach followed the New Orleans Mayor de Lesseps "Chep" Morrison and his wife through the door. Marie met him there.

"Hello Zach. My, but don't you look handsome," She reached up and placed a soft kiss on Zach's cheek.

He smelled her perfume once again. His heart soared.

"You're looking beautiful as ever," responded Zach; and he administered a kiss to her delicate hand. Pausing, he looked up with a devilish grin and released her.

"Zach, this is Mr. and Mrs. Morrison. And this is Zach LaSalle, a student and basketball player at Tulane." All parties shook hands.

" You all had a good season this year."

"Pretty good. We just couldn't get past Kentucky."

"A lot of people can't get past Kentucky."

The mayor and his wife were intercepted by Baron Antoinne. "Hello Chep."

"Hello Tony." They moved off amidst gesticulation and small talk.

Marie continued to meet the guests, and Zach wandered into the cavernous double parlor. Pete Daily's Dixieland Band played a subdued version of the "Original Dixieland One-Step." Lighthearted banter amongst the ever-increasing number of party-goers continued to build. The air felt festive and exhilarating.

A couple finished dancing a blurred version of the Lindy Hop and Charleston to the band's "Sensation Rag." Pete Daily's cornet led the band in a biting rendition of the "Dixieland Shuffle."

"Say Cowboy, could a lady have this dance?" Marie, who else, sauntered over to him. They eased into a Fox Trot.

Zach could dance. He was energetic, light on his feet, and had a feel for the music. He and Marie made a striking couple. People turned to watch as they passed. The dance ended.

"I could dance all night with you," said Zach as he pulled

Marie closer to him.

"There will be another one or two," she said, before gliding toward the bandstand where she talked briefly with Pete Daily. The band moved into their next number. "Careless Love." Zach recognized the number. Was he Marie's careless love? While giving this serious contemplation, a complete stranger tapped him on the shoulder.

"I am Jacque Buisson, Marie's fiancée. I believe you must be Zach LaSalle. Pleased to meet you."

A surge of adrenaline hit Zach. So this was the guy in the Black Buick. Zach sized him up. Dark, handsome and suave. "Yes, I am Zach LaSalle," as he forced himself to return, "nice to meet you, too."

"Marie has told me about you—this Texan from Dallas. So you like New Orleans and going to school at Tulane?'

"It's great. I love it," countered Zach. How come Jacque knows about him? And Marie didn't tell him about Jacque?

"I must tell you, my man, that Marie belongs to me. You are just whistlin' Dixie with her. Nevertheless, all is fair in love and war, enjoy yourself tonight, young buddy." Jacque excused himself and joined in the fun and gossip nearby.

Young Buddy! Where does he get this Young Buddy stuff? So this was his competition. He wondered if he was in over his head.

The band struck a chord, and Tony led Marie over to the band. Party-goer voices grew muted.

"And now as a special treat for the evening, may I present my beloved, your beloved, Marie Tranchepaine."

Marie wore a fitted elegant black dress that complemented her raven black hair and soft dewy skin. She moved her head gracefully back and forth to the band's introductory chorus of "Bye Bye Blackbird."

> *Pack up all my cares and woes,*
> *Feelin' low, here I go,*
> *Bye Bye Blackbird.*
> *Where somebody waits for me,*
> *Sugar's sweet and so is he,*
> *Bye Bye Blackbird.*
> *No one seems to know or understand me,*
> *Oh what hard luck stories*
> *They all hand me.*
> *When somebody finally shines my light,*
> *I'll be coming home tonight,*
> *Blackbird, Bye Bye.*

The band picked up the melody and continued playing. Zach finished the number dancing with Marie in his arms. He had never felt closer to her, including the night in her chamber. He didn't care if Jacque had said she belonged to him. After the band concluded "Bye Bye Blackbird" they started "My Sweet Embraceable You." Zach continued to hold Marie, and they began another dance together. A quite recognizable tap came to his shoulder.

"Excuse me," and Jacque cut in and moved away with Marie.

Soon Zach completely lost sight of the pair. He heard a lively animated conversation taking place in the corner of the parlor.

"How is your book coming along, Mr. Williams?"

"Progressing very nicely," responded Tennessee Williams. "I have been in your enchanting city for about six months. It is a very inspirational place to write."

"Have you named the book?" queried the inquisitive lady in a chic dress and matching headband.

"Not yet, maybe something to do with streetcars. This place

abounds with them."

They did not include Zach in the conversation, but he listened attentively. After all, his English professor had told him to pay attention to the immediate situation.

Pete Daily's band struck up "What's Your Story." Zach was making his.

The party revelers were engrossed in an orgy of self-congratulations of clever conversation and inching closer by the minute to a dining table that waiters had recently wheeled into the parlor. Mardi Gras colors adorned the table – purple for justice, green for faith and gold for power. The menu for the evening lay enticingly arranged.

Pommes de terre soufflé,
Rockefeller, Foch, and Bienville oyster dishes,
Trout with pecans,
Shrimp clemenceau,
Sweet potatoes,
Fried green tomatoes,
And, for dessert:
Cream caramel.
Lemon crepes
Peppermint stick ice cream.
Delicieux!

Zach and other guests helped themselves.

After eating far too much, Zach wandered into the Baron's game room and encountered individuals squatted down in the corner throwing dice.

"Le crapaud!" came a beleaguered voice. It belonged to Jacque. He had shot craps.

Zach shook hands with Tony who stood watching nearby.

"What is 'le crapaud'?" inquired Zach.

"An old French game of throwing the dice in a crouched position. *Crapaud* is French for frog. If you sit around on your haunches like a frog and throw the dice, you have a game of *crapaud.* Thus, shooting craps."

Zach knew better than to join in. He had a one-dollar bill in his pocket.

He could hear the rich and mellow refrain of "I Want to Linger." He could smell the magnolias. Where is Marie? He wondered.

At that moment, she slipped her hand into Zach's. "You do remember, don't you." They left the other men to their craps and slowly dipped and glided around the parlor.

"When do we put on our masks?" asked Zach.

"At the midnight ball at the Fairmont Hotel."

Zach looked at his watch. 11:30 p.m. "Marie, am I invited to the ball?"

"You surely are."

Are you going with me, or Jackass?"

"You mean Jacque." Marie smiled. "He is so busy shooting *le crapaud* he may miss the ball. Do you have an offer?"

"Do I have an offer! How about a ride in a special blue limo with a man who has the private *munificence* of one dollar in his pocket."

"I'll get my coat."

My bounty is as boundless as the sea.
My love as deep.
The more I give to thee,
The more I have.
For both are infinite.
--William Shakespeare. Romeo and Juliet. Act II Sc. 2, Ln. 133.

Chapter 19
▼ ▼ ▼

Other guests began to leave as Marie and Zach pressed through the front door. A Tranchepaine never left the house through a rear exit. A light drizzle fell as they hurried around to the back of the house.

"There's our blue limo," announced Zach with an air of foolishness.

"Where? I don't see a limo anywhere."

"Here." Zach pointed out his Blue Goose pickup.

"You gotta be kidding me."

Zach inserted the key in the passenger side door, opened it, and bowing expertly said, "Allow me, Your Highness."

Marie had changed into a long evening dress. She lifted her dress ever so gingerly and stepped up into the pickup. The seat felt firm, and she detected a faint scent of gasoline.

The Blue Goose's carburetor delivered a very fresh mix of gas to the V8 engine.

"Where in the world did you get this thing?" questioned Marie.

"What do you mean 'thaing'?" asserted Zach with mock

indignity. "This might well be the best ride you ever had." He pulled the truck onto St. Charles Avenue and headed toward the Fairmont Hotel. Slap, slap went his driver-side windshield wiper. The passenger side wiper lay dormant.

Lack of a wiper on Marie's side severely restricted her ability to see. She sat back in the seat and laughed uproariously. "Zach, you're just full of you know what. We do have a littering ordinance in New Orleans."

Zach laughed with Marie. "This is probably the most fun you ever had." An impish grin followed this remark.

"There is a first time for everything, and this is my first pickup date. No pun intended." Marie's sense of humor showed in her smiling eyes.

The Blue Goose transported this fun-loving duo nicely to the Fairmont Hotel. Zach let Marie out on the University Street entrance and went in search of a parking place. He put his mask in his hip pocket, locked the Goose, and joined Marie waiting for him in the opulent lobby. The lobby walls were finished in a matte black. Red velvet furniture with gold accents formed conversation areas around the immense marble floor.

Marie left her coat in the cloakroom and proceeded with Zach to the entrance of the ballroom. The captain of the *krewe* required Marie to show her identification as a *comus*. She and Zach then entered the ballroom. Marie and Zach donned their masks and began dancing to the Rex theme song of the ball, "If Ever I Cease to Love You." The party was in full swing with the Dukes of Dixieland providing the music. The *comus* King, Queen and Dukes sat upon a raised platform at the end of the room.

Marie spoke to Zach over the din of music and noise. "That's the *caste of tableaux."* She pointed to the King's party.

"The what?" asked Zach.

"Never mind, we're getting ready to march. Get in line and to my right."

The Dukes struck up the King Zuzu Parade and the King and Queen led the revelers around the room full of strut and pomposity. Zach joined in and did a little strutting himself.

After the march, Marie and Zach joined the *tableaux* in a back inner sanctum for toasts and champagne. Zach found large quantities of wine and liquor available. He indulged in the champagne. What a night.

Marie and Zach stood off to the side and visited with Tony and Julia Calve.

"Are you enjoying the evening, Mr. LaSalle?" inquired Julia.

"I've never seen anything like it, but coming with Marie definitely made the price of admission worthwhile." Zach wondered why he said that. He hadn't paid for anything yet. "I don't understand any of this, but it is big-time fun."

Tony offered this explanation, "The *Comus Krewe* dates back to 1857. Even Frenchmen had to wait awhile to join. This is our Mardi Gras Ball, which takes place on 'Fat Tuesday' 41 days before Easter and the season of Lent. Simply stated, we can raise hell for a while before it comes time to repent. *Comus* comes from the Greek word *komos,* which means reveler. Julia was a *comus* queen in 1939. Hasn't been another one as pretty since."

Julia hoisted her champagne glass to that.

"I hadn't had a chance to thank you for the invitation." Zach raised his glass. "Here's to the Tranchepaines. May they reign forever." Zach had become slightly loose and tipsy. He was unaccustomed to alcoholic beverages and had no tolerance.

He noticed that Marie and Julia wore similar necklaces. "I must say, I admire your necklaces."

"They have been in the family for years. We only wear them on this special occasion."

Zach's feet grew fidgety. Brother Frank and Fred Assunto were leading The Dukes of Dixieland who were pumping out a soulful and expressive, "Down in Honky Tonk Town." Marie and Zach were at their best jiving to this beat. Marie couldn't contain herself, and on a Lindy Hop, she kept on solo hoppin'. Zach loved her rhythm. Others stopped to watch Marie's special interpretation.

Zach felt a shove in the back, and someone pushed him to one side. It was Jacque, who moved in on Marie, caught her by the wrist and hustled her off the dance floor.

"I looked all over for you at your house. Did you come here with him?" Jacque pointed to Zach who, with hands on his hips had moved closer to Marie and Jacque.

Marie had anticipated things might get out of hand if she invited Zach, but she hadn't wanted to dismiss him. His raw sexuality and easy-going manner had left their mark. However, Jacque hadn't quite taken to Zach, for obvious reasons. On top of that, she could tell he was drunk.

Zach held his ground. He didn't like being pushed in the back by Jacque but, on Marie's behalf, he didn't want to make a scene. However, he wasn't going to take anything off of Jacque, even for her.

"Where I come from, you dance with the one that brung ya'. Do you have a problem with that?" He and Jacque stood nose to nose.

"We'll see about this later, Monsieur Zach." Jacque glared at Marie and brushed past Zach.

Marie rolled her eyes and thought she had bitten off more than she could chew. She was relieved that Jacque had moved on. In times past this could have resulted in a pistol duel in the "dueling park." Thank goodness men didn't shoot each other anymore. Still danger laced the air. An explosion could happen any time. She was, after all, Jacque's woman. What to do about Zach? It was a *conundrum*.

Zach took her arm, and they danced to "Do You Know What It Means to Miss New Orleans?" He held her close.

"I want you," he whispered.

"I want you, too," she replied, shocked at the truth of her statement. Was it Zach or the excitement of the moment? She didn't know, and she didn't care. They finished the number and Zach pulled her from the ballroom. He gave the cloak girl the small round tag with Marie's coat number on it.

"Here it is. Look carefully; lots of fur coats in here tonight."

"Yes, this is it. Thank you."

" Wait at the door, and I'll bring the 'limo' around."

Zach looked awfully good as he disappeared quickly out the door.

"Are you going home with him?" Jacque strolled up behind her.

"Yes."

"You'll be sorry." Jacque's face grew livid with rage, but he controlled himself with great effort, spun on his heel and returned to the ballroom.

Marie heard a couple of toots from a very weak horn. Zach drove up. She could see him grinning through the window of the pickup. She loved his smile. She found it infectious.

He pushed the passenger door open and, this time, she hopped in, dragging her dress in behind her. She slid across the seat until she could feel her hip against Zach's. It was a rainy cold night in New Orleans.

Zach shifted the gears on the Blue Goose. When he dropped the gear back down into third he patted Marie's knee and left his hand there. She reached up for a kiss. Her lips felt soft and moist, like a peach. Marie knew how to cocoon a man and meet his every need. He found her presence compelling, and Zach could not resist her, even if he had wanted.

They didn't speak as he drove down St. Charles Avenue. It was the wee hours of the morning. One wiper vigorously smeared the rain on his windshield. Damn, he needed a new wiper. He turned the truck into the driveway at the back of Marie's house. It was dark, except for a faint street light flickering through the mist. The rumble of the Blue Goose exhaust went silent as he turned off the key. Zach pushed the gear up into second. He turned to Marie, and their lips met with fury and passion. Desire swept them into a wonderful wild longing.

Zach's hands circled Marie's hips, pulling her toward him. They paused. He helped her out of her gown. The rest, she did unaided. Off came Zach's coat and shirt. The heat of their bodies quickly fogged up the windows. With no barriers, they explored each other.

Nothing mattered to Marie except the feel of his body against her. They matched each other skin on skin. Zach was a big man, and he took up most of the pickup seat, but he was inventive and now accomplished.

"Are you my shining light?"

"Yes, and I've come home tonight."

Dancing a loving rhythm, their movements brought sheer joy. Moments later, the cosmos exploded. They were as one in the universe.

Zach cradled Marie in his arms, breathless and at peace. He pulled her coat up around her shoulders. The streetcar clanged by. It ran 24 hours a day. They had christened the Blue Goose.

The inevitability of parting was upon them. Zach walked her to the front door and finished the night with a gentle kiss on the forehead. Marie's lips looked full and slightly swollen. He soothed them with a final kiss.

"See you tomorrow," said Zach.

"Ah, yes, call me around noon." She could hardly get the words out.

Zach walked back to his pickup in his rumpled tux. Now there were two nights that he would never forget.

Chapter 20
▼▼▼

With little sleep to their credit, the Tranchepaines rose in time for coffee and to attend Early Mass. During church services, Marie's thoughts drifted back to last night's affair. She had made love in Zach's pickup. It had been wonderful.

Martin picked up the Tranchepaine family after church services concluded and whisked them back to 1938 St. Charles Avenue. Liz fixed light sandwiches for the family lunch. Seated around a small table in the dining room, Julia spoke first in a disapproving manner.

"We missed you last night for the final parade of queens. You were not to be found."

"I left a little early, Mama."

Tony joined in. "Did you leave with that LaSalle fellow?"

"Yes. I left with Zach. Why are both of you so concerned? After all, you are talking to a 20-year-old woman."

"People were talking about that scene with Jacque. It was, after all, quite inappropriate," said Julia, following a sip on her coffee. "Mr. LaSalle appears to be a fine young man, but he is hardly your type – or better, a Tranchepaine type."

"And what would constitute a Tranchepaine type?" asked Marie, her voice laced with sarcasm.

"Jacque Buisson," scored Tony.

"Oh, in heaven's name," declared Marie, who left her chair and moved toward the parlor.

"Marie, we need to talk," said Julia, imperatively. "This ballplayer Texan of yours is hardly grown-up. Hardly a man."

Marie whirled and came walking back in a resolute manner. "Hardly a man?" A slow mischievous grin spread across Marie's face.

"Would you have more coffee?" inquired Liz.

"Yes, please." Marie had again seated herself at the table. "I am more confused than you are. I will admit, in hindsight, that it probably did not make a lot of sense to invite Zach and Jacque to the same party."

"You need to give Jacque a date for the wedding," admonished Julia.

"We are not engaged now."

"Jacque sure as hell thinks you are," added Tony, who shared immense business interests with the Buisson family. "You and Jacque are perfect for each other. He has his business degree from Tulane and could give you the kind of life you deserve. As a matter of fact, he and I drove out to the area of the old Valcour Aime plantation, and he showed me where he wants to build a house for you. The Buissons own a good part of that cane country over in St. James Parish."

"Yes, I know. Jacque has taken me there several times. It is a pretty area."

Julia lit a cigarette contained in a jewel lined holder. "Jacque is well educated, handsome, suave, rich and –well—like us."

"Like us, Mama?"

"Like us – French."

"Zach's last name is LaSalle."

"But not a New Orleans LaSalle," said Julia with eyebrows raised.

"Zach is not exactly black-eye peas and cornbread. He is an interesting mix of laid-back stoic intellectualism, musical ability, athleticism, fun, and well – he strikes a chord in me that rings my bell."

Marie had a very open relationship with Julia and Tony. The three of them rarely spared their feelings and attitudes about things with one another.

"It's your life, sweetheart," said Tony as he stood up from the table and stretched. "Be careful in what direction you head, as you might end up there. Zach may be this young Renaissance man, but do you really want to end up with a basketball coach or college professor?"

"Zach and I communicate on so many different levels. I think I do love Jacque, but this 'Dallas Cowboy' is giving him a run for his money."

"It's unfinished business, my dear," said Julia as she disappeared into the parlor.

Tony gave Marie a hug. "Be careful, Baby."

Chapter 21
▼▼▼

Back at the dorm that morning, Zach wrestled with his conscience. Should he go to church, or not? The devil won out, and Zach sacked in until noon. He ate his Sunday dinner meal in the dorm, and then gave Marie a call.

"Hello, Tranchepaine residence," said a cheery Liz.

"May I speak with Marie, please," responded Zach.

"May I tell her who is calling?"

"Zach LaSalle."

"Just a minute, Mr. LaSalle."

"Hello, Zach. I assume you and the Blue Goose made it home okay this morning."

"Nothing to it," said an assuring Zach. "How about a caffy olay and a baig net this afternoon?" he queried.

Marie had gotten used to his horseplay. "I've been drinking coffee all morning. But believe I have one more cup in me. Make it at 3 p.m. I'll be ready."

"See you then."

Fatigued from the night before, Marie took a brief nap in her boudoir.

She was awakened when Liz gently patted her on the shoulder. "It is Mr. Buisson. He insists on talking to you. He is waiting on the phone."

"All right, Liz. Thank you. I'll take the phone in here."

"I wanted to see if you were home. I'll be over in a few minutes."

Before Marie could respond, the phone went dead. She knew that Jacque would be at her door just as he had said. Things were getting out of hand. Tony had said to be careful.

She was still groggy from her nap as she emerged from her bath. Her gilded clock under bell cover struck 2 p.m. She reached for her towel and was wiping down when Jacque appeared in her sitting room. She felt strangely violated. This was uncharacteristic of Jacque. He spoke not a word. His eyes were smoldering. Marie wrapped her towel about her and approached Jacque. "If you would be so kind as to wait in the parlor, I will join you in a minute."

"Where is he?" questioned an agitated Jacque.

"Where is who?"

"Your boy basketball player." Jacque stood accusatory and threatening. " He spent the night and early morning with you. You're playing games with me, Marie, and I don't like it one damn bit. I'll wait for you in the parlor."

Jacque paced the parlor floor, and soon Marie appeared.

"You are acting so childish, Jacque, and besides what I do is my business and none of yours."

"I'm making it my business. Can we go for a drive?"

"Not this afternoon, Jacque. I am tired. You can, however, pick me up after school tomorrow—say around 4 p.m. I will meet you in the library."

Jacque approached Marie. "You know how much I care." He leaned forward taking Marie in his arms. She felt stiff. Under pressure, she yielded an auntly kiss.

Marie heard the parlor clock chime on the half hour. Must be 2:30 p.m. Zach would arrive soon. She walked Jacque to the door.

"See you tomorrow," and kissed him on the cheek.

A blue pickup, trailing a slightly bluish gray haze from the exhaust, traveled north along the avenue. The driver, Zach LaSalle, had decked out in his Levis and boots. He wore his favorite corduroy western shirt. Life was good he thought as he fiddled with a sometimes working radio. He wanted a little background music. All he got, however, was static. Zach looked up from the radio in time to catch a glance of a dark convertible as it whizzed by. The car looked familiar. He turned his head for a better look. The pickup cab blocked his view. He pulled into the entranceway and stopped his pickup in front of Marie's home. It backfired, then quit running.

"What was that?" said a sleepy eyed Julia arousing from an afternoon nap.

"Sounded like a gunshot to me." Tony got out of bed and looked out his second story bedroom window. "Julia, would you come here and look at this."

The Blue Goose stood out in grandiose ignominy.

Marie was on Zach's arm. Their gestures were spontaneous and accepting. He opened the door for her and slammed it shut. A couple of long-legged strides put him in the driver's seat. He fired up the Blue Goose and tried to shift from first to second. The gear hung. He double clutched and with a lurch it released, sending Zach and Marie out on the avenue in a cloud of smoke and glory.

Julia and Tony stood dumbstruck at the window. Tony turned to Julia. "Damndest thing I ever saw." And they both laughed.

Chapter 22
▼▼▼

Marie cozied up to Zach as they turned onto Canal Street and looked for a parking space. With the Blue Goose firmly entrenched along the curb, Marie and Zach began their walk to the *Café du Monde*. Zach sensed Marie's confident stride as they held hands walking down Chartres Street. Their body language evidenced their feelings for one another. Once settled into their seats at *Café du Monde*, Zach ordered the obligatory *beignets*.

"Let's have some hot chocolate. Whataya' say, Zach."

"Sounds good to me."

Marie leaned toward Zach. "Andre needs a second trumpet player in the pit band down at the Palace. Would you be interested?"

"Mama Kate's Andre?" responded Zach in a questioning manner.

"You may not know, but Andre owns and operates the Palace Theatre."

"No kidding. In addition to the Acme."

"No kidding. I told him you played a pretty mean trumpet, and I would talk with you."

"What a treat. Yes I'll do it."

"Do you think you could begin this coming Thursday? With the spring and summer season coming on, we are going to a Thursday, Friday, Saturday night venue."

"I'm sittin' on ready," said a cocksure Zach.

"Showtime is 8 p.m. The boys in the band begin to warm up around 7 p.m. I suggest you get there at 6:30 in order to become acquainted with the situation."

"Well, I'll be with you on those three nights. You can't beat a deal like that."

"We better head back to the Goose," cautioned Marie. "Those clouds over the lake look bad."

They took last sips of chocolate and headed back toward Canal Street. The wind had picked up, and an early spring storm seemed imminent. Marie always had her trademark New Orleans umbrella handy. A few drops began to splatter the sidewalk. Marie opened her umbrella, and she and Zach huddled underneath as they hurriedly made their way back to Zach's pickup. Zach sank his key into the lock. Click, and the door opened. They both crawled in. The rain came down in sheets.

"This may be one of those frog-stranglin' gulley washers, Marie."

"New Orleans gets more rain than any place in the country; and being below sea level doesn't help any,"

"I never have understood where the water goes."

"The levees keep it under control while big old pumps go to work pumping the water over into Lake Ponchatrain."

"Marie, you know everything." An unmistakable feeling of love engulfed Zach like the rain obliterating his view of the road.

His one and only windshield wiper was against the downpour.

The water was rising rapidly on St. Charles Avenue, and Zach, with his head slightly out of the window, slowly inched his way toward Marie's home. Zach negotiated the familiar driveway and pulled up in front of her house.

They made a run for the porch. Marie's face was dripping wet with her dark hair forming small ringlets across her forehead. Zach took her face in his hands, and their lips touched lightly, then firmly. The kiss grew long and passionate.

"Please come in, Zach."

"Don't mind if I do."

Marie shook out her umbrella and pulled her hair back from her face. She could not have been more beautiful, thought Zach.

"Anybody home?" called out Marie.

"Yoo hoo," came a reply. "We are in the study," echoed Julia.

Classical music played softly in the background. Tony, with reading glasses resting down on his nose, looked up as Marie and Zach entered the room.

"Come in here and get dry. Quite a rainstorm we have out there, and it's not letting up. Have a brandy, Zach?"

"Yes, thank you." There is a first time for everything, thought Zach, and this would be his first Sunday afternoon brandy.

With drinks in hand, Marie and Zach joined Tony and Julia.

"Won't be long until you two scholars will wind up the spring semester," Tony casually remarked. "You going to be around this summer or go back to Dallas?" he asked Zach.

"I had thought about going home this summer, but Marie may have gotten me a job playing down at the Palace. If it works out, I think I may stay in New Orleans." Zach looked engagingly at Marie as he talked.

"Have you told Zach about your plans to go to France this summer?" Julia asked Marie.

"Not yet, but I had planned to soon."

To France! This hit Zach like a ton of bricks. "France," he said with eyebrows raised. He looked straight at Marie.

"Yes, it is part of my last class in French literature. Traveling abroad is part of one's education. Care for a game of eight ball?"

"Rack 'em."

Marie broke the triangle. One ball fell. She positioned herself for her first shot.

"You didn't tell me about this France stuff," said a slightly agitated Zach.

Marie sank her third ball. "No need to cross a bridge until you get to it."

Marie missed her fourth shot.

It was now Zach's turn. He studied his options and decided upon a chop shot with reverse spin that would run a ball down the side of the cushion into a corner pocket. "My bridge has already been crossed, Marie. As much as I look forward to playing at the Palace, nothing could keep me in New Orleans this summer but you. You are New Orleans. It's all wrapped up in my mind together."

Zach's shot fell neatly into the corner pocket.

Marie studied Zach. She didn't like the possessive tone in his voice. As a matter of fact she didn't like that in any man. She craved her independence.

"Jacque and I had planned to be married this spring, and the trip to France would have been part of our honeymoon. Zach, my boy, you really complicated things."

Zach rammed a ball in a side pocket. "Is that what I am—a complication?"

Zach missed his next shot, but left Marie with a poor lie.

Marie put her stick down and moved toward Zach, encircling her arms around his waist. "You are much more than a complication, my dear. I do love ya', but I just don't know if I am in love with you, or Jacque for that matter. I will go to France this summer. Maybe I can sort things out over there. We can be lovers, Zach, without being in love."

Zach gently parted from Marie and looked away. She was so fresh and open to depths he had not yet explored. Winning Marie would not be an easy task. She was not a woman to be conquered; but he was on a learning curve maybe to steep too climb.

"I probably better go."

"Let's finish the game. Zach."

"Oh, I don't think so." Zach had a sinking feeling in the pit of his stomach.

"I'll fix us a sandwich. You need something on your stomach after that brandy."

" No thanks, Marie."

Zach poked his head in the study on his way out. "Nice seeing you all again," he said to Julia and Tony.

"Nice to see you, too," responded Tony. Julia waved and turned back to her book.

"What numbers are you going to do this Thursday?" asked Zach, attempting to mask his feelings.

"'Bye Bye Blackbird', for sure," said Marie.

"See you then," Zach forced a painful grin.

Zach drove back to the Tulane campus bewitched, bothered and bewildered.

Chapter 23
▼▼▼

Zach spent the next several days studying for his final spring semester exams, shooting pool with his basketball buddies and getting his lip in shape practicing on his trumpet in the band hall. Thursday rolled around and Zach, trumpet case in hand, strolled down the aisle of the Palace Theatre. A couple of players in the pit band were casually running scales.

"Hello, I'm Lu Watters. I play lead cornet. You must be my new sidekick on second cornet. Or is that a trumpet you have in there?"

"Pleased to meet ya'. Zach LaSalle; and yes this is a trumpet."

"A trumpet is a bit too mellow, but it will have to do. Ever play this kind of music?" Lu asked as he pointed to some sheet music folded neatly on music stands.

"I played some Dixie, and think I will have a pretty good feel for the music," responded Zach.

"Bob Scobey usually plays second cornet, but he is out on the West Coast and can't make it back for a while. The word is that you are pretty decent," said Lu in an encouraging fashion.

Other members of the band began to appear. Turk Murphy on trombone; Wally Rose, piano; Ellis Horne, clarinet; Clancy Hayes, banjo; Russ Bennett, banjo; Dick Lame, tuba; and Bill Dart, drums.

Zach had remembered from Marie's instructions to wear a white long sleeve shirt and black bow tie. He settled in with the rest of the band. The house lights dimmed. The band took their seats highlighted with an incandescent glow from attached lights to music stands.

"It's Showtime, boys. 'Muskrat Ramble' here we come." With measurable rhythm, the band eased into this oldtime ramble, and the mood was struck. With the curtain down, the footlights brightened the stage. Zach had played lead trumpet on "Muskrat Ramble" many times. This was his first attempt as second trumpet, providing harmony for Lu Watters. He found the experience exhilarating. What a rush. Zach had his music sequences set before him. After the warm-up of "Muskrat Ramble", the show opened with the Red-hot Babes in long dresses, bloomers and parasols strutting and cakewalking to "Smokey Mokes".

"Smokey Mokes" was new to Zach, and he had to follow the sheet music. The other band members knew it by heart. He had to look up and find Marie. His eyes settled on her where she danced, in the middle, twirling her parasol and smiling to beat the band. Zach's heartbeat quickened. The Babes turned and flashed their bloomers to the delight of the crowd. They then did a chorus line kick off the stage, and the Master of Ceremonies ran out in striped blazer and straw hat. The usual repertoire of corny jokes ensued. Zach thought he would like to try MC'ing some time. Right now, he had his hands full with "Smoky Mokes."

A tenor took the stage and belted out a stirring rendition of "When Irish Eyes are Smiling."

"Wasn't that pretty?" intoned the MC when they finished. "Let's bring Eddie Savage back. Here he is with that old favorite, 'The Blarney Stone'." Zach waited patiently through the number. The Irish tenor finished and moved backstage amidst splattered applause. But insincere applause is better than none at all.

"And now, ladies and gentlemen, a feast for sore eyes, and your entertainment pleasure, a special presentation tonight. Here she is: the incomparable, the beautiful, the scintillating Miss Kate."

The spotlight shone on the center of the curtain that slowly rose with the band pumping out "Memphis Blues." Zach took a deep breath. It was Kate Robicheaux. He watched and hit an occasional right-sounding note. Time had gently etched its presence on the Quarter's premier dancing queen. However, it didn't matter, as it was a dance for the ages. Kate was aglow in feathers, sequins and satin; and finished her dance with class and flair to thunderous applause. She picked up a stray feather and teased with it as she quickly moved off stage.

As Kate departed the stage, the band struck up the "Original Jelly Roll Blues" and the scantily clad Red-hot Babes took the stage in a pulsating rhythmic dance. They were all sensational, but Zach only had eyes for Marie. She saw him in the pit and blew a kiss.

Acrobats and jugglers followed this routine, and the night wore on to the concluding number.

"Ladies and gentlemen for your great pleasure we have saved the lovely – the talented – the dazzling – the sensuous Marie Tranchepaine for our final number. Here she is – my favorite, and yours."

The spotlight shone brightly on Marie, dressed in a long black gown. The band played an introductory chorus to "Bye Bye Blackbird." Marie sang it like nobody else could. She found Zach and focused on him with glistening eyes. Heaven would have to be something to be better than this, thought Zach. He entered a dream state. Marie received a standing ovation and a long stemmed rose from the MC. She quickly exited and the band struck up its closing number "Irish Black Bottom Rag". Zach's lip had gone numb, but he gave it all he had.

This show, with minor variations, repeated countless times during the months of March, April and May. During those months, Zach and Marie were inseparable. Zach completed his schoolwork at Tulane and prepared to attend Marie's graduation from Loyola University.

Chapter 24
▼ ▼ ▼

Zach, among many others, seated himself in a chair placed on the lawn for graduation exercises at Loyola University. Marie would receive her Bachelor of Arts degree on this fine spring day. Dogwood blossoms redolently perfumed the Loyola campus. The landscape unfolded around him laced with pink ruffle azaleas, a profusion of ferns, purple dawn, peppermint camellias, red roses, yellow hibiscus and white magnolias. The sun shone brightly, further enhancing the beauty of the scene.

A brass ensemble began the proceedings with a traditional graduation march. Somber academicians, trappings denoting rank and degrees attained, followed the mace carrier and the university president in their walk toward a raised platform. Family members and well-wishers turned in their seats in order to secure a better view. Master's and bachelor's degree candidates followed the faculty and took their seats in front of the raised stage.

Zach spotted Marie just before she took her seat. After announcements and the awarding of an honorary doctorate, the president spoke to the pending graduates.

"I should like for each of you today to ask yourself as you leave Loyola: What truths, beauty and goodness am I taking away from here that I didn't bring with me? What new strengths do I have that were not mine when I came? Have my personal ideals been lifted? Am I in better control of my instincts and appetites? Have my intellectual and cultural vistas broadened? Do I, more than ever before, enjoy association with the great minds and hearts of ages past? Am I reluctant to judge and criticize others lest my own house fail to be in order?

"During these years, as I have worked in the laboratory and library, as I have listened to the lectures in the classroom, and as I have participated in student activities, have I come to feel a higher respect for truth and to love more its manifestations in nature and in man? Is human personality more sacred to me now than formerly, and do I respect it wherever found?

"If, candidates for graduation in the class of 1947, any or all of the questions can be answered affirmatively, you and the faculty can be most proud, for Loyola has done its job. And you are entitled to bear the mantle of an educated person."

"Will the candidates for the Bachelor of Arts and Bachelor of Science degrees please rise?" intoned the academic dean.

"According to the faculty of Loyola University, you have met all of the requirements for the degrees for which you are entitled. By the authority of the board of directors and the president of Loyola University, I hereby grant these degrees to you. You may move your tassels from the right to the left. Congratulations, graduates of Loyola University."

After the awarding of master's degrees, the ceremony concluded with the singing of the alma mater.

Tony, Julia and Marie's friends circled around her. As Zach approached, he couldn't fail to notice that Jacque stood with his arm around Marie. He caught her eye. She lingered with a look, and then turned away. An overpowering feeling that he stood outside her circle of friends and admirers overcame Zach. It hurt.

Instead of joining the group as he had planned, he turned away and walked down a flagstone promenade flanked on either side with sparkling fountains and old-fashioned benches. He sat down on a bench in order to collect his thoughts. An overgrown purple trumpet vine provided some shade.

The perfume caught Zach's attention instantaneously as Marie sat down beside him a few minutes later. She took his hand and looked at him.

"Why did you leave?"

"I'd rather not say."

"Zach, you mean so much to me, and I do love ya'." Marie said importantly. "I'm leaving for Paris next week, you know."

"I know. Will Jacque go with you?"

"It is unsettled. Zach, it's not the end of the world."

Zach couldn't hide his feelings. "Maybe not for you, but it is not that easy for me to be separated from you."

Marie leaned forward and sweetly and tenderly kissed Zach. Their lips lingered and when separated, Marie stood up. "I'll be seeing you, Cowboy," she said confidently.

Zach wasn't so sure. "Goodbye, blackbird."

Marie returned to her family and friends and Zach walked dejectedly toward the Blue Goose.

He thought of these lines by Hjorth Boyesen in Gunnar, which he had recently memorized in his literature class.

Love is like fire,
Wounds of fire are hard to bear,
Harder still are those of love.

Chapter 25
▼ ▼ ▼

Zach finished up his junior year's work at Tulane and decided to remain in New Orleans for the summer. Marie made her way to Paris. Whether or not Jacque accompanied her, Zach wasn't sure. The thought tormented him, when he let it. He missed her, especially during the performances at the Palace. He continued to play second trumpet in the pit band. Next to Marie and basketball, this was his love. It was a hoot. Zach had taken a small apartment in the Quarter. He paid for it with wages earned at the Palace. The dormitory was not open at Tulane during the summer. He wanted to visit his folks in Dallas, but the trip took time and money, and he wasn't sure the old Blue Goose would make it there and back. He didn't have travel fare for a train trip.

Zach called Liz at Marie's home and obtained Marie's mailing address. He addressed the envelope.

Ms. Marie Tranchepaine
Café Guerbois
Grande Rue des Batignolles
Paris, France

Inside the envelope he wrote:

Dear Marie,

Summer in New Orleans is sure hot and sticky. Wish I could cool off in your bath. The shows at the Palace are going okay. Would be a lot better if you were there. Oh well, things are never like they should be; only rough approximations. My greatest wish is to meet the requirements of my imagination with you. I am living life sufficiently, but with you it could be exceptional. You are my lucky star.

I love you, Bird.

Zach

Zach waited and wished for a reply, but none came. Had she received his letter? If so, did she even care enough to write him? He had made sure she had his new address in the Quarter. Had something happened to Marie? He would go to France to see her. But not on the $10 he had in his pocket. She had said, "I'll be seeing you, in my dreams." That's what it was. She would only see him again in her dreams, and he was destined to only be with her in his.

In late August, Zach still had not heard from Marie. He drove by her house, repeatedly. Maybe she had come home. According to Liz, she had not. If he could only have one sweet letter from her. But none came.

Chapter 26
▼ ▼ ▼

After midnight on a hot late August night, George Jirard fronted Phil Zito's New Orleans International City Dixielanders in a stirring rendition of "Bye Bye Blackbird." George finished his vocal…

*Make the bed and light the light,
And I'll come home tonight,
Blackbird, bye, bye.*

Zach's favorite trumpet player then lifted his silver horn to his lips and drove the band home with its particularly vigorous brand of New Orleans Dixieland Jazz. Phil Zito, at drums, led the pulsating rhythm section comprised additionally of Emile Christian on bass, and Roy Zimmerman at piano. Pete Fountain had his clarinet held high and punctuated Jirard's trumpet note for note. Joe Rotis pulled everything together with his rasping and gliding trombone.

Out of the corner of his eye, Zach caught the silhouette of a dark-haired lady entering the Famous Door. Zach could make out a lavender dress and fuchsia hat. It had rained on this evening, and she shook droplets of moisture from her hat and umbrella. She threw her head back. Even though he knew better, Zach's heartbeat quickened. She turned, came forward, smiled at Zach, and seated herself.

No, it was not Marie. How could it be? How foolish of Zach to think otherwise; Marie only existed in his dreams. He paid for the one beer he had nursed through two sessions and moved outside to a steamy hot night in the crescent city. The sound of Zito's band faded as he walked slowly to his apartment thinking of Marie, and lines by Sir Thomas Browne came to him.

> "In your arms was still delight,
> Quiet as a street at night,
> And thoughts of you I do remember.

Three months later Zach read in the paper of Marie's engagement to be married. A gut-wrenching pain overwhelmed him. The inevitability of losing Marie was confirmed; this was the end of their story. But what a story it was -- Zach would never be the same. Marie had taught him about women, New Orleans, culture and about life. She brought him from advanced boyhood to manhood, and for that he would always be grateful. He would look back on this time in his life with fond memories, but he would always have a touch of the Bourbon Street Blues.

▼ ▼ ▼

Epilogue
▼ ▼ ▼

Zach finished his college studies, coached for awhile and served as an officer in the United States Air Force. He later completed graduate work, became a family man, and a university professor. His passion for Dixieland jazz remained and the New Orleans experience etched in his soul a feeling for the blues that made him him a pretty darn good musician.

Marie lived in Paris for a short time and returned to New Orleans. After a failed marriage, she made the "big time" in Hollywood as a singer and dancer.

Printed in the United States
47236LVS00002B/169-216